I0593882

Praise for
K.C. HILTON'S WORK

Praise for
MY NAME IS RAPUNZEL

1. "I recommend this book to anyone who wants to believe once again, if only just for a little while. Fairy tales can come true!"

2. "This book was very good. It had a very different twist on the story of Rapunzel. I'd like to see a movie based on this book."

3. "The beginning got me into reading this book, and the ending was why I liked it so much. I really love Rapunzel's tale and I really enjoyed this version of it."

4. "This book was everything I expected and more. I have read many fairy tale books and stories and quite a few on Rapunzel, but none with this sort of outlook or twist. The plot is so riveting and unusual, that you feel compelled to go back and read the story a second time."

5. "My Name is Rapunzel by K.C. Hilton is a beautifully written fairytale retold by a great author who knows how to keep her readers on edge. I liked this book a lot. I felt like I stepped into the time of fairytales, dragons and witches myself. It was so imaginative!

Praise for
THE FINKLETON SERIES

1. "This is by far, the best novel I have read all year, and if I could have given it ten stars, I would have."

2. "She is truly a genius in her mad writing skills, and this book portrays to all audiences who love a little magic in their life."

3. "Fans of fantasy, adventure, time travel, and magic will enjoying reading this book."

4. "Young readers, prepare to find a comfortable spot on the edge of your seats."

5. "If ever a series of books deserved to be made into a movie look no further than the Finkleton series by KC Hilton."

Advance Praise
CARS, COFFEE, AND A
BADASS NINJA TOILET

What does a toilet have to do with your book?
~My Neighbor

Can you read it to me?
~My Friend

It'll move like ex-lax. Just push a little harder.
~Same Friend

I should've bought the fucking hutch.
~My Husband

She was short and that saved us money on her
casket.
~The person reading my eulogy in the future.

Actual Praise
CARS, COFFEE, AND A
BADASS NINJA TOILET

A joy to read, an absolute page-turner, and a
cautionary tale for anyone who thinks being
in business for yourself is easy—it isn't.
Most highly recommended.
~J. Magnus for Readers' Favorite

A rollicking read, humorous, and filled with
drama; a book that keeps you in your seat for
long hours and that fills you with laughter.
~D. Zape for Readers' Favorite

A fun and entertaining read. The writing style
is very engaging and creative. I appreciated how
K.C. Hilton has highlighted the inherent gen-
der bias and sexism that she encounters being a
female boss in a predominantly male dominated
field.
~G. Dixon for Readers' Favorite

A laugh-out-loud comedy about a female car dealer fighting against stigmas and sexism. This is a hilarious read starring a semi-hysterical badass female ninja. I loved this book! It was so funny!

I appreciated how the author showed the difficulty in Julia maintaining a balance between her work life and her home.

~A. Elmore for Readers' Favorite

A rather amusing and interesting read. It gives you plenty of reasons to laugh out loud—literally speaking!

~K. Anisi for Readers' Favorite

.

CARS, COFFEE,

and a Badass Ninja Toilet

A JULIA KARR NOVEL *by*

K.C. HILTON

CARS, COFFEE, AND
A BADASS NINJA TOILET

Published by Book Boss Publishing
Cover Design by The Killion Group Inc.
www.theKillionGroupInc.com

© 2018 by K.C. Hilton
www.kc-hilton.com

Print ISBN-13: 978-0999334515
Print ISBN-10: 0999334514
LCCN: 2017911614

Cover Design and Interior Format

ALSO BY K.C. HILTON

The Magic of Finkleton
Return to Finkleton
90 Miles to Freedom
My Name is Rapunzel
Cars, Coffee, and a Badass Ninja Toilet

(COMING SOON)
Cars, Coffee, and a Slightly Used Casket

Dedication

I want to thank my loving husband for supplying me with as much wine and chocolate as I desire. He doesn't mind it when I vent about the crazy shit that happens throughout the day. That's true love.

I especially want to thank those people who drove me crazy, gifted me with everlasting anxiety, and helped me find new wine flavors to enjoy. Without them, this book wouldn't have been possible.

And to the bastard who cut me off this morning—You, sir, are a total dick.

Acknowledgments

Special thanks goes out to a great bunch of people. They wanted to know what life was like owning a business and encouraged me to write a book about it. Through their shock and fits of laughter, I knew they were right. I will be forever grateful for their suggestions, honest feedback and support.

Contents

Preface

A FULL DISCLOSURE

People dream about owning a business, making tons of money and living the American dream. I'm living proof that it doesn't necessarily work that way. Owning a business gets in the way of real life. I used to dream about all the money we'd make, the vacations to faraway islands with my husband and taking a day off whenever I wanted. All the romantic possibilities of being my own boss! I never fantasized about the sleep deprivation, chasing down overdue payments, or jumping cars in the rain and snow. The sacrifices are real; very real. You've been warned. Full disclosure.

I own a car lot with my husband. Sounds pretty straightforward until you consider that cars are a unifying commodity. Almost everyone needs a car. Other businesses have it easy. Someone selling sporting goods would have a bunch of athletes for customers, or a garden shop would attract mostly gardeners. They at least have a rough idea of who's headed their way. But on our lot? We get every brand of strange and outrageous available.

I can at least say it's not boring. But between chasing thieves, fighting for respect, dodging runaway cars, and fielding wild requests, my blood pressure could use a break.

Seeing the business world through my jaded eyes may convince you that owning a business isn't what it's cracked up to be. I'm a car dealer with monthly periods, no matter how irregular they are. My attitude is drenched with sarcasm and dipped in crazy sauce. I blame the car lot.

Chapter One

COUNTING PENNIES

"I'm done with this fucking car lot, Romeo. I'm over it!"

Those were the words I flung at my husband last week. I was on the verge of a major breakdown. It happened sometimes. Especially when owning and managing a used car lot, dealing with customers all day, every day—in person, on the phone, through email, through text, you name it. It never stopped.

It was growing official. My breakdown-to-keep-going ratio was looking like shit. Some days I had to make an appointment with my toilet just to go to the bathroom. And forget about taking lunch! My keyboard full of crumbs could attest to that. It was getting to the point that I didn't want to answer the phone. My brain was so drained at the end of the day that cooking dinner or doing household chores was the last thing I wanted to do. But I still did it because I was a super-ninja wife.

My husband Romeo and I owned a used car lot. We had attended some public auto auctions when we were first dating and bought some vehicles to repair and sell for extra cash. We never intended to become small business owners and we certainly didn't see ourselves opening a car lot back then. But by the time we got married, that's what had happened. Something that had started out as a hobby had turned into a full-time business.

"I'm at the end of my rope," I said, as I sat on the end of the bed, Romeo holding my hand.

"It'll just take time to settle down, you'll see."

"Time? I've given it fifteen years!" I ripped my hand from his—a clear sign I was in full-blown meltdown mode. Romeo took a deep breath.

"What do you want, Julia?"

It was hard to put into words. I wanted the phone to stop ringing all day, I wanted customers to respect me, and I wanted to feel good.

"We can fix this. You just need to relax a little," Romeo suggested.

"Relax!" I shouted. Romeo was always understanding, but he should have known that would set me off.

"Okay, okay," he said. "Not relax. Something else."

"We sell everything," I said. I felt a smile coming on just at the thought of it. "All the in-house contracts. Everything. Shut the business down." I chuckled. I was giddy to say it aloud. Shit, I'd even apply to work at McDonald's if I had to. It had to be better than this. Plus, I'd get french fries.

"Slow down," Romeo pleaded. "Okay. I hear you. Let me think about this. I'll come up with a solution."

It took poor Romeo an entire evening to calm me down and talk me out of quitting. My brain was nothing more than a goddamn clusterfuck.

I used to see the good in people and believed that what they told me was true. I used to go that extra mile to help people when they needed it. But, mostly they took advantage of my kindness. Now I was fed-up, done with it. I was done with all the lies and the lack of full disclosure. I was done with the rude and demanding customers that called and acted like their problems were mine. Customers like the Windshield Wiper Lady.

A few days ago, I sent Windshield Wiper Lady a friendly email reminder that her monthly payment was late and to please go online and make the payment to bring her account current. The customer replied with a long, detailed email explaining that she was upset about having to buy windshield wipers. She didn't expect to have to spend money on a car that she had only owned for six months. Not only was she upset, but she demanded to know what I was going to do about it.

What I wanted to tell the customer, but couldn't, was if a ten dollar set of windshield wipers from Walmart was going to set her back, then she probably shouldn't own a vehicle. When it was time for her car to have an oil change, or tires, or a battery, she would be SOL. She didn't understand that vehicles were machines. And machines need maintenance.

Windshield Wiper Lady emailed me the next day and said she couldn't afford to make her payment and asked if she could split it up over the next two months. If I agreed, then she'd never be late again. Well, I've heard that story before and more often than I'd like to admit. Instead of arguing through emails, I caved and gave her a chance to prove my psychic abilities wrong.

I've been there before; I knew life could be cruel sometimes. But I also knew sad stories didn't pay the bills. This car lot had changed me and turned me into someone I didn't know. To be honest, I didn't like the woman staring back at me in the mirror.

I wasn't even getting a paycheck. We were running the lot to make sales and build the business up. We wanted the business to act as an investment for our retirement. Everything got reinvested back into the cars and the damn lot.

Romeo knew me better. He knew I wouldn't quit. I'd just had a shitty day. Unfortunately, it wouldn't be the last.

Romeo had come up with a plan by morning.

"I've got it, Julia. We sell some of the contracts. Keep some, sell some."

I sprang to his arms. To preserve my sanity, my awesome husband decided to ease some of the tension. Let another lender deal with people like the windshield wiper lady. Though it meant we had to part with some great customers, and I hated to give them up, it did help cut down on some of the stressful customer service work.

Romeo worked as an electrician all day, so that morning I kissed Romeo goodbye and wished him a good day at work, then watched his huge badass truck pull out of the driveway. Armed with a cup of coffee in one hand and my phone in the other, I headed to work myself. Thirty-five steps were all it took before I arrived at the office door. In theory, living next to our business was supposed to give me the freedom to do other things during the day. Things like doing a load of laundry, walking the dog, or even taking a few sips of wine to help with a bad day. But finding time to do those extra things was becoming harder and harder.

Owning a business a mere thirty-five steps away had some big disadvantages. We had a life outside of the car lot, but some people didn't care or respect that. Like the person who knocked on our door early one Christmas morning and asked about a car while the kids were opening their gifts. Needless to say, Romeo didn't offer him any eggnog.

My day started out right and I felt better about Romeo's agreement to sell off some of the contracts. But I still needed something to do to take my mind off the stress of the car lot.

During an unexpected and rare lunch hour, I visited Lowe's. A storewide sale was going on and I needed a project, or an idea for a project. I really wanted to remodel our entire bathroom, but we were a long way off from that.

A few months ago, I told Romeo I wanted to remodel the bathroom in style. "And how, exactly, do you suggest we pay for this dream bathroom?" Romeo asked. Of course we both knew we didn't have the extra money. I scooped up some loose change off the counter and dropped it into a coffee mug with a clink. "Penny by penny," I said.

Romeo smiled and emptied his pockets into the same mug. "You got it."

We were more than a few mugs full of change away from being ready for the remodel, but I needed to do something. Besides, a new coat of paint would be cheaper and easier to do. So I selected a handful of paint swatch samples in hopes of finding one that I could live with.

After returning from lunch an older man came into the office and asked about a few cars we had for sale. The gentleman wanted to surprise his wife with a new used car. He didn't need a loan and wanted to pay for it in full. Hallelujah! I loved selling cars to people who didn't need financing because it was less paperwork. The best part about selling a car straight out meant I wouldn't have to deal with stupid complaints or hunt a customer down to collect past due payments. I was on cloud nine.

I gave the customer a great cash price and included a free 90-day warranty. He asked about the brakes and I told him they could stop on a dime. For some reason the customer started laughing. He laughed so hard he started coughing, then finally stopped to catch his breath and wipe his eyes. I didn't understand why he laughed so much. I went over our conversation in my mind a few times, but I couldn't figure it out. He probably thought I said something else, so I just brushed it off. Bottom line, he was happy and I was smiling. It was a win-win.

The customer shook my hand and said, "I need to go get the money. I'll be back, soon."

I handed him a card and replied, "Okay, I'll be here."

About an hour later the gentleman returned to the lot. I was in the office doing some boring paperwork when he came in with a five-gallon bucket. He set it down with a thud in the lobby area, then made several more trips out to his car and each time he returned lugging another five-gallon bucket—six in all. I had a bad feeling about what was going to happen, but I didn't dare move from my seat until he was finished hauling all those buckets inside.

The customer plopped down on a chair on

the other side of my desk with a plastic grocery bag bulging full of something that my x-ray vision couldn't detect. His breathing was heavy and I chided myself for not helping him. "I've been saving for a long time," he said.

I glanced nervously as my eyes bounced back and forth between him and the buckets in the lobby and asked, "Saving *what* exactly?"

The customer laughed between a few coughs. "All of my change." He then gestured toward the buckets like a proud father, "We'd better start counting. I don't want to short-change you."

I was at a complete loss for words. There was no hiding the confusion painted all over my face. The customer laughed again, then walked over and picked up a bucket and brought it to the side of my desk. I peeked inside and noticed it was about halfway full of quarters, nickels and dimes. I was blown away. Change Man plucked a dime out of the bucket, placed it on my desk and started laughing again. "Can we test those brakes out?"

I looked at Change Man, then raised my eyebrows in question. "Don't banks have change counting machines?"

Change Man pointed to the plastic bag. "My bank said I'd be charged a fee, so I accepted a bunch of free coin wrappers instead."

"Great," I said, forcing a weak smile and trying my best to look happy. At the end of the day, money was money, no matter what form it was in. I couldn't complain. Besides, I was a car dealer and car dealers boldly go where no salesperson has gone before. Some dealers accepted cell phones, televisions, computers or dogs (depending on the year, make and model) as trade-ins. Now I would be added to that noble list of unusual dealers, because I accepted buckets of loose change.

Two hours later, Romeo arrived home from work and came to the office to see if I needed help with anything. He stopped in his tracks and did a double-take when he noticed the buckets of mixed change in the lobby. Romeo looked at me and raised an eyebrow.

There was nothing I could I say; the buckets said it all. It was all I could do to keep from laughing.

I smiled and asked, "How was your day, Honey?" Before Romeo had the chance to answer, I pointed toward the buckets, "We could use your help."

"With what exactly?" Romeo shifted. It looked like he was ready to bolt and make a run for it.

Change Man interrupted our conversation with a broad smile and held up another coin wrapper, "Counting my change. I'm buying a car."

Romeo slumped his shoulders in defeat, but he didn't object. Instead, he pulled a chair over from the lobby, then cleared away a section of my desk and dug right in. With Romeo's help, the sorting, stacking and filling of the coin wrappers went a lot faster. Excitement surged through me when we started on the last bucket, and I did a little happy dance in my chair.

"We are on a roll!" I said. "A coin roll that is."

Change Man laughed along with me, but Romeo didn't.

"Oh come on," I said. "You thought saving coins for the remodeling was a great idea." Romeo smiled, but was obviously tired and grouchy from reading blueprints, pulling wire or running electrical conduit at work all day. He was a trooper though—he'd be okay.

After the coins were counted, it took me less than twenty minutes to print all the forms and complete the sale. Romeo removed the advertising from the vehicle and handed the keys to Change Man. I wasn't looking forward to making this deposit at the bank.

It was just after midnight when we were finally able to lock up and go home. Thankfully, Change Man gave us the five-gallon buckets, free of charge. My fingers were cramped, my stomach was growling, and my brain was exhausted. I had a bad feeling I would probably dream of being locked up in a prison and sentenced to counting endless amounts of change for the rest of my life.

As Romeo held open the door to our home, I announced, "I don't want to save anymore change." Romeo nodded his head in agreement.

Unfortunately for me, if the buckets of change went, my dreams of the bathroom remodel went with them.

Chapter Two

HOBBITS LOVE CHOCOLATE

Romeo found a great lender to sell the contracts to, and it took me an entire morning and skipping my lunch break to get everything together and send it to them for pre-approvals. It gave me a reason to like these cold, rainy days when the lot was usually slow.

I called our customers to explain the transition. Many were excited, one was slightly confused, some ignored my calls and emails, and two didn't want their contracts transferred. Seemed like no problem.

But then the lender needed to do phone verifications with each customer to verbally confirm their identity and to make sure we weren't lying through our teeth, I supposed. I didn't understand why the lender had to do verifications when we submitted all the information they requested along with signed contracts, which clearly showed we had the right to transfer contracts to a third party.

"All the paperwork's in order," I said. "Don't you think verifications seem redundant?" Translation: they're a total waste of my time. But when in business mode, I was super-ninja polite.

"Doesn't change what I need on my end," Lender Man said.

I tried not to lose my temper.

"Mortgage companies don't ask for permission to transfer home loans to a different lender. Why bother with a little thing like a car?" I challenged.

"Houses are harder to hide and they don't move around," he said with a bored voice.

Okay, good point Lender Man. He had me there.

I finally understood why businesses transferred contracts and took a loss on the amount due because we were trying to do the same thing. Our business could expand and flourish into something bigger using the money from the buyouts. The only change our customers would experience would be to who and where they mailed their payments. No big deal, or so I thought.

The lender e-mailed me a list of the transfers, and more than half were marked "Unverified." Maybe that was to be expected since most people worked during the day. Besides, I didn't like to answer strange 800 numbers calling my phone either, and I didn't expect our customers to be any different.

More work for me. So I picked up the phone and started making calls to all the unverified customers and sent emails, too. The first number I called was to a cantankerous man who didn't give a shit about our business. He probably thought we had a ton of money and we hated him and that's why we wanted to get rid of his contract. Only the latter half was true.

"This is a win for both of us," I said.

"You mean just for you," Grumpy Man replied.

I rummaged through my desk drawer. There had to be a chocolate in there somewhere: a cure for jerks like him. He just didn't understand and refused to believe a word I said.

"I have a contract with *you*." His voice boomed through the phone. "You want to change that, then I'm getting my money back."

"I'm sure the new lender could…"

"I'll bring my vehicle back. And a lawyer,

too," Grumpy Man interrupted.

I didn't want to piss off a good paying customer, even though he was being rude and disrespectful.

"We'll be happy to keep your contract in-house, then," I said. My jaw clenched in a smile, even though there was no one to see it. So I would deal with his shitty attitude for the next two years. Two years. This type of customer was the foundation for high blood pressure, nervous breakdowns, and medication.

After I hung up the phone, I buried my face in my hands and chanted over and over, "Think happy thoughts. Think happy thoughts. Chocolate. Wine. Chocolate. Wine." Thinking didn't help. So I chose the real thing.

I'd had enough of being yelled at that morning, so I decided to go to donut shop next door. Chocolate could make a hell of a difference on days like this. Wine worked too, but I had several hours before I could close for the day. Besides, chocolate was much cheaper than a therapist and the end result was the same. Maybe one day, my health insurance company would thank me for saving them money.

Then I remembered the air cast. I fractured my heel jumping in and out of some of the taller trucks on our lot. The monster-size trucks were so high people really needed a stepladder to get in or out of them. Especially if they were vertically challenged like me. I thought a ninja auto dealer wouldn't need one, but it turns out my fractured heel did.

Romeo referred to me as "Hobbit-sized." I seriously enjoyed *The Lord of the Rings* but I took a little offense to being called Hobbit-sized. Not that Hobbits weren't super cute, but I believed I was of average height: five foot, two inches. I was normal. Romeo begged to differ. It wasn't my fault over half the human race inherited some form of tall-alien DNA and grew like Jack's beanstalk.

If I really wanted to blame someone for my injury, it would be the fashion industry. The extra two inches on my jeans were just enough to trip me up on the hop and land with a fracture. Some years ago, someone decided to categorize vertically challenged people, such as myself, as short or petite. That was so not fair. First of all, I was over five feet, not under. Besides, the short and petite clothes didn't fit me right. The average-size jeans fit me better in my hips and thighs, except for being a football field too long.

That was why jean sales went down and comfortable leggings had taken over the world. If the jean companies took surveys and read my social media complaints, then they would have remained competitive in the market. I've given up trying to help giant consumer product companies. It's their loss, not mine.

Anyway, I hobbled with my Hobbit-sized leg in an air cast toward the donut shop. There was no cute way to walk around in a medical boot that restricted certain movements. Worst of all, it wasn't even pink.

If I had to be stuck wearing this burden all day (the cast really helped the pain by the way, so kudos to my doctor), then I should be able to at least make a fucking fashion statement. I'm not some fashionista, but I should at least be offered clip-on changeable colors or something. Instead, I wrapped it with a pink scarf to give it some class.

After a chocolate donut or three, I took my time on my way back to the shop. Chocolate boosts were often tragically short-lived. I was thinking of how I ought to try re-branding petite sizes. Perhaps a new Hobbit line would be the million-dollar idea to get me off this lot. My cell phone interrupted my train of thought with a forwarded call from the business line. I hoped it was the jeans people calling. It would be totally awesome to finally get recognition for my ideas. Regretfully, it was just another customer with a question. I had to put my dreams of riches on a brief hold, but without that annoying elevator music.

"I'm calling about the black Toyota you have on your lot," a man said. From the road noises I heard in the background, I could tell he was driving.

"The Camry?" I asked. It was the only black Toyota we had on the lot for sale and I wanted to make sure he wasn't talking about another black vehicle.

"No," he replied. "It's the two-door Toyota Solara."

We got this a lot. People drove by and called instead of taking the time to stop and actually look at a vehicle. Usually, what they thought they saw ended up being an entirely different car. "I'm sorry, we don't have a two-door Toyota Solara."

"Yes, you do!" The customer yelled through the phone. "It's in the front row. It has two doors, and it's black. I just drove by and saw it!"

On the phone, people tended to have more guts and fury than when they stood face-to-face with someone and had to be respectful. It was time I put this guy in his place, but in a nice way of course. "Well, we have two Toyota Camrys. They both have four doors. One is black, and the other one is gray."

"What about the black Jeep, huh?"

"I'm sorry," I replied in a sugar sweet tone. "We don't have any Jeeps at this time."

"I must have the wrong car lot," the caller mumbled. And without an apology, he hung up the phone.

"Screw chocolate," I said out loud. I needed some fucking wine. And I had some serious research to do into patents if I ever wanted to get away from this lot and move away from Stupidville.

Chapter Three

I DON'T PLAY WITH DOLLS

A few days later, I found myself on a step stool with my head under the hood of an old truck, basking in the grease on my elbows. I'd rather be deep in grubby grease than inside the office typing, answering phones or doing paperwork—frivolous stuff. My hair was wind-blown and my pink t-shirt and jean shorts were so filthy I contemplated throwing them away. I could only imagine what my face looked like since I had wiped the sweat away with my hands instead of using a shop rag, not that it would have been much better. At least my pink running shoes were still clean. I looked kind of awesome, actually. Sure, I'm a girl and I wore pink—it was my signature color—but I had a job to do.

You would think that my loving husband Romeo would be the one topping off the fluids in the vehicles, but that's not how things rolled on this lot. He worked hard enough during the week. Besides, I wasn't the type of woman who was concerned about wearing make-up or breaking a manicured nail. I didn't mind airing up tires or hooking up a jump box to a battery in the dead of winter. Our car lot wasn't going to run on its own.

I finished what I was doing, stepped down from the stool and started filling gasoline jugs. Left to my own devices, I started daydreaming about household chores needing to be done, what to cook for dinner and the homemade ice cream waiting for me in the freezer. My train of thought was disrupted by the sound of an engine shutting down.

I hadn't noticed a vehicle pull onto the lot, so I was taken aback when I turned and saw a beautiful, tall woman step out of her car. All dolled up with make-up like the perfect Barbie, she flipped her long blonde hair over her shoulders, batted her eyes, and looked around the lot. She definitely wasn't here to buy a car.

Finally her gaze landed on me and she began walking in my direction. I wouldn't have taken much notice of her red high heel shoes if it weren't for the click-click-click-click sound they made as she walked on the pavement toward me. I bit my bottom lip to keep from laughing at the sound.

"So, is he in?" she asked in a high-pitched, flirty voice. Oh no, she didn't just say that. It took everything I had not to snap my fingers and draw the letter Z in the air. Nope, Barbie wasn't here to buy a car. I knew it.

I reluctantly stopped what I was doing (I was seriously having fun filling those gas jugs), wiped the gasoline off my hands, and took inventory of what I must look like to her. My clothes were dirty, I was covered in grime, and I was filling up gasoline jugs. I forcibly brushed away my feelings of inferiority. After all, I couldn't wear heels for this job and actually get rough-and-ready car lot work done at the same time. I stood a little straighter and pulled my shoulders back—there was no way I'd magically grow as tall as her. I didn't know how to respond. So, I looked this woman in the eye and replied with pride, "I am he."

Was my response a little too smug? Perhaps. Was I acting a trifle arrogant? Definitely. But teaching Barbie a lesson was going to be *priceless*. Don't get me wrong. I was polite, over-polite, in fact. Her flirtatious smile faded away and mine grew extra wide. Barbie had planned to use her gorgeous looks and seductive manner as part of her sales pitch for whatever it was she had come here to sell. I wasn't born yesterday.

"Oh," she said. "I'm here to speak with the man in charge. I have a great advertising opportunity he'll want to hear about."

Wow, she was really dense.

"Yeah, you'll talk to me about that."

"I was hoping to talk with the owner."

I sighed. "Yeah, that would be me."

She flashed another big smile then. Too late, Barbie. I'm sure that particular sales tactic works well on men, but I also know that confidence, knowledge, intelligence, and hard work go a long way to gain the respect of others. In this day and age, no matter how beautiful a woman is, she should know better than to simply assume only a man can run a car lot, or any other "male" business for that matter.

In spite of the strides we owe to the feminists, a car lot is a business still widely run by men. Usually, from men, I got behavior and comments that showed they assumed that only a man could run a car lot. I battled with that attitude every day. But this was the first time it happened to me with a woman.

Beautiful Barbie would have been shocked

if I told her the truth about me—if I told her that I wanted to learn to be a mechanic and that I already owned several pink tools. Would she have fainted if I told her I was a master barber? I bet she would have had a coronary if I told her I used to risk my life as a volunteer firefighter with the county fire department. I could see it in her face, her mouth hanging open in shock, as if to say, "a woman running a car lot and doing a man's job—how scandalous." Give me a fucking break. Better yet, give me the respect I deserve. I've earned it.

What I really wanted to tell Barbie was that she just had the privilege of meeting a strong and independent woman—one with a brain—a woman who works as hard as any man, yet still knows how to be pretty and feminine. I wanted to tell her that she just met a woman who cooks and cleans, loves her family, and—oh yeah—a woman who can run a car lot as well as any man can. I don't need to wear stilettos or show cleavage down to my waist to prove something. At the end of the day, I've worked hard, and I can be proud of what I have accomplished. Romeo is proud of me too. And really, that's all that matters.

I know other women like me, who do "a man's job," and we have much in common. Strength, pride and intelligence unite us in a bond of supportive understanding. It's a wonderful feeling—priceless, in fact.

After Barbie left with a bemused look on her face, I logged into my social media account to tell everyone I knew to take heed the next time he or she approached a woman in any business.

"Don't assume she isn't the one in charge. Don't assume she isn't the boss or owner of the establishment. Most of all, give her the respect she so rightly deserves. Just because a woman is taking calls, vacuuming floors, washing cars, or filling up gas jugs, doesn't mean that *she* isn't the *he* you're looking for."

I logged off and felt inspired. I grabbed my pink tool kit and got to work on some small repairs. I had a battery to replace and some spark plugs to swap out on one of our vehicles. After dealing with Barbie, these normally tedious tasks felt amazing. The lot may have been wearing me down, but I also knew part of me grew stronger for it.

Chapter Four

♡

PROJECT TIME

Owning and operating a business had taken over our lives, so if I could find the time to do anything outside of the business, I was all for it. Anything worked, like going shopping, doing a project, or destroying something so we had a project. I had a history. There was the dishwasher meltdown, the time I pounded a hole in the living room wall while trying to hang something, and no one let me forget the time I "fixed" the TV and we had to get a new one. But—for the record—it really was our dog, Foxy Boxy, who chewed up a two-foot section of linoleum in the middle of the kitchen floor. I swear I didn't do it. Girl Scout's honor. After the linoleum was ruined, Romeo installed a new wood floor that I'd been wanting. My dog is fucking awesome.

Some days I just wanted to forget about the car lot altogether. When I did, my imagination goes into overdrive and home projects are born—like the bathroom update I'd had on my mind. Romeo didn't like my projects and it was usually a good idea that he wasn't home when I started them.

It was a slow day, so during my extended lunch break, I went back to Lowes to get some more inspiration. Television shows about flipping houses made DIY projects look so easy.

I walked out of Lowes with some new cabinet knobs, sticky tile flooring and paint. I couldn't wait to start on our bathroom, but I was hungry. I needed some fast food, fast. The kind of food I could eat while driving. As soon as I thought of it, the golden arches of McDonald's emerged, and my stomach grumbled with anticipation. I licked my lips at the thought of devouring some hot fries and got in the drive-through line.

"Looks like the card machine's down," the manager said. "Got any cash?"

I giggled a little at the question and replied, "Who carries cash anymore?"

The manager laughed, too. "It's your lucky

day. Your meal is free."

The only thing better than getting a front parking spot at Lowe's was getting a free meal at McDonald's. I'd hit the fucking food lottery.

I was doing a little happy dance until I noticed the McDonald's manager standing mere feet from me in the drive through window. So I just smiled and smiled. The bathroom was going to get a face-lift and I got free food. This day was turning out to be awesome. In the back of my mind, I hoped nobody would call or come by the lot to fuck it up.

Before I could pull my vehicle forward, the manager turned away from the window and yelled, "Cash only, people! The machine is down!" I'd bet someone else's money that McDonald's lost a ton of sales during that lunch rush.

I pinched a potato morsel from my bag of freebie food and savored the crunchy taste as I drove home. It was the little things that made my day.

I dropped off the supplies at the house, and when I returned to the lot, I was bombarded with customers and phone calls. Somehow I didn't mind. I had a belly full of free food and I was going to tackle the bathroom DIY-style before Romeo got home. I could hardly wait to surprise him.

♡   ♡   ♡

Romeo was surprised, that's for sure. I was cooking dinner when he walked through the door to see all the paint and tile just sitting where I had left it on the kitchen floor. I didn't have a chance to do anything to the bathroom, since the car lot kept me busy all afternoon. Not my fault. "What's all this?" Romeo inquired.

I smiled and eagerly rubbed my hands together, "I'm going to give the bathroom a face-lift."

Romeo rolled his eyes and placed his lunch box on the kitchen table. "Julia, you and your little projects always turn into major repairs."

I didn't want a major project, just a little something to do. "It's just some paint and the tile is sticky. It won't be hard to install."

"There's nothing easy about installing tile, sticky or not," Romeo said.

It was true most of my projects started with simply changing out a light fixture or a faucet, but they had to start somewhere. It wasn't my fault we ended up fixing or replacing other things during a small project. Finding wires that led to nothing or wondering why someone stole the insulation from an outer wall were just happenstance. No one should build a house and forget to install insulation in the outer walls. It had to have been there at some point. Stuff just happened to make my projects grow larger, but my intentions were always good.

Since my surprise wasn't a surprise anymore, I decided we should remove the cabinets and vanity to paint the bathroom properly. And it would be easier to lay the new tile, too.

Romeo pulled up the old linoleum and inspected the floor beneath it to determine if we could use the peel and stick tile. He found a bad area in the sub-flooring, then turned to me and raised an eyebrow. That adorable thing he did with his eyebrow was never a good sign. It was all I could do not to laugh. He was just so darn cute when he got irritated. I winced.

"Sorry," I said.

Romeo mumbled a few curse words and took some measurements. A few minutes later he decided to go to the local lumberyard and purchase some plywood.

When he returned, he set the receipt on the table.

"This 'little project' is growing expensive," he said.

"I got free McDonald's today, so every-thing's balanced!" At least I could still make him laugh when he was grumpy.

We ate dinner, then he proceeded to remove the bad section of floor. Aside from the old plywood being screwed down, it was also glued to the joists, which caused Romeo to curse even more. Replacing that bad section of plywood took at least two hours. Good thing I made dessert.

After repairing the floor, Romeo wiped his face on his sleeve.

"With the floor fixed," he said. "It might be the best time to replace that old shower." At that moment, I thought I heard angels singing.

"Let's do it!"

It was already a joint remodeling venture. I worried about the extra time and cost, but since he suggested the additional update, I was all for it. Our bathroom was going to get more than a face-lift. Yes!

Romeo and I went back to Lowes to price shower inserts. At the corner of the bath and shower area, an end-cap advertisement for a Champion 4 toilet made me stop and catch my breath. The advertisement read: "Champion 4-Flushes 16 golf balls in a single flush." I was in awe. I never knew how badly I wanted to flush golf balls down a toilet. We didn't need a new toilet, but this was the mother of all toilets. A toilet's gotta know its limitations, but the Champion 4 had none. That advertisement made me want to test that shit out.

I used my cell phone to take a photo so I would have proof of that awesome display and show all my friends on social media. Then I searched YouTube and found lots of visual proof of its magnificent flushing powers. I lingered below the super toilet display, watched a few videos and daydreamed about owning one of those super flushers.

Strangers walked passed me, obviously hearing the sounds of a toilet flushing over and over through my phone with the volume on full. I briefly forgot I was in a public place.

Romeo found me glued to my phone, beneath the awesome toilet, "Julia, what are you doing?"

I pulled my eyes away from the whooshing video and pointed up toward the toilet advertisement. "I want to buy 16 golf balls to see if our toilet can do that, too!" I shoved my phone in front of his face at the exact moment the video showed 16 golf balls being flushed down the Champion 4 toilet.

Romeo took a step back, then looked at me and said, "You've lost your fucking mind." Romeo didn't have a spontaneous persona.

"Aren't you just a little curious to see if we own a badass ninja toilet that could flush 16 golf balls?" I asked as my legs did a little happy wiggle.

"No," Romeo said, then walked away and left me standing there, with my imagination running wild. I stood there in silence, gazing up at the Champion 4 toilet, wondering if I could test the badass flushing capabilities of our toilet at home without Romeo ever knowing. I lived for moments like this.

I could see it clearly: one day in the future, Romeo would pull me close and whisper in my ear to tell me how awesome I was for appreciating the fine art of the Champion 4 turbo-flush technology. Then I would reply, "Let's go flush some balls together." It could happen. Either way, I had the urge to flush some golf balls.

Good ads are supposed to make consumers want to test things out and make sure the advertising isn't lying. For instance, if my detergent label stated that I could wash 32 loads of laundry, then I expected to wash that many loads or more. If I bought one dozen donuts, then I expected twelve donuts, not eleven. Advertising people needed to take a lesson from the Champion 4 toilet display because damn, it was awesome. I believed it could change my life—in a toilet kind of way.

Romeo escorted me away from the ad.

"I'll miss you," I whispered over my shoulder to the Champion 4. Romeo rolled his eyes.

The bathroom was finally void of all cabinet and vanity obstructions, but we left the toilet in place. I found myself gazing down at the lonely toilet and wondered how it must feel. I felt sad for the little guy. It had been loyal to us all these years and never once complained about seeing our butts and flushing shit day after day. It didn't have an exciting life and I wanted to be the person who changed that. I wanted to give our toilet a name.

My search engine friend, Google, found a ton of stuff for me to ponder about. For instance, Sir John Harrington invented the first flushable toilet. But Thomas Crapper, a famous plumber, manufactured the first widely successful flushing toilet. I loved Google. It just taught me why some people referred to the toilet as "The John" or "The Crapper." Knowing that bit of information will give Romeo and me something else to talk about during dinner. I was sure he would find it just as interesting as I did.

From this day forward, I bestowed the name of Sir Johnny to our toilet. It totally worked. No Champion 4 toilet was going to get in the way of Sir Johnny becoming the next super flusher. I needed to buy some golf balls to bring some excitement into his porcelain life. Golf balls and maybe a toilet light, so Romeo could piss in the dark.

"Once we do this, there's no turning back, Julia," Romeo said as he held a hammer ready to strike and destroy the dividing shower wall. "Any regrets?" Romeo asked.

"Not one! You are go for launch." No one seriously wanted a 1970s avocado-green shower. Romeo looked happy to get rid of it, too. The way I saw it, this project would bring us closer together, and not just because our bathroom was the size of a large closet. There was no better way to spend time with the person you loved than working on a project together.

Romeo removed the old shower and discovered that the water lines were installed wrong. He shook his head and stared at the screwed-up plumbing, "Seriously, who runs water lines around the two-by-four studs instead of through them?"

I inspected the copper plumbing, where Romeo indicated the problems. I started documenting all the weird discoveries with the camera on my cell phone. When it comes to working on our home, nothing surprised us anymore.

The water lines had to be redone before a

new shower could be installed. So that meant I had to contact a plumber, because Romeo said he hated plumbing and that was why he became an electrician. He made sense, but in all honesty, electricity could kill people and water just gets them wet.

I wanted to get Romeo's mind off the bad plumbing, so I picked up a hammer and asked, "What's a ball-peen hammer used for, except for making circle dents in the wall when I miss the nails?"

"It's for hitting ball-peens," Romeo said with certainty, while he examined the pipes.

His answer confused me even more, "What's a ball-peen?"

"I have no idea," Romeo replied without care. He didn't want to be bothered with my silly questions. But maybe, it was because he didn't know the answer.

For once, Romeo didn't know the answer to something: a rare event in my experience. I was going to make it a ninja mission to find out the answer. I only had so much time to find the answer before Romeo needed the funny hammer back.

Google told me the ball-peen hammer was made for use in striking and shaping metal materials. It was also used for hitting chisels and punches. In the past, the peening hammer was used for the manufacturing of swords and knife blades.

I bit my lip and refrained from doing a happy dance. We owned a hammer that could make a sword! That was so freaking cool. I scribbled on a sticky note to remind myself to Google "badass ninja people with swords." I could totally learn a new trade and become a secret ninja—like the turtles, but in human form.

The ball-peen hammer made swords, not lightsabers, so becoming a Jedi Knight would be totally out of the question. I'd have to settle for being a ninja.

On a medieval naming roll, I dubbed the ball-peen hammer "thy Sword Hammer." From that day forward, Romeo and I would say, "Hand me thy Sword Hammer, please," or "Where is thy Sword Hammer?" Women should be in charge of naming tools. They'd have much cooler names.

We made a trip to a locally owned family hardware store for something Romeo said we needed for the bathroom remodel. While he was busy locating what we went there to buy, I browsed around the store.

When I got to the end of one of the aisles, I found used golf balls for sale in zip-lock bags. I stopped myself from doing a happy dance in the middle of the hardware store because I saw a kid pointing his cell phone at me, and that shit would end up going viral on social media. The kid could have been taking a selfie, but I wasn't taking any chances.

I pulled out my cell phone and took a photo of the bags to forward to the cereal people and post on social media. If golf balls were sold in zip-locked bags, then cereal could be too.

I squealed with excitement and that was enough to get Romeo to look in my direction from two aisles away. Romeo could easily see over the aisles to find me waving my arms like a mad woman. "Look! Golf balls for the badass ninja toilet experiment! It's an omen."

"No," Romeo replied. "It's not." And he continued the practical things he was doing. Some days I swore that man had no imagination. I don't know how he didn't see the advantages of knowing if we owned a badass ninja toilet or not. To an outsider, it might have looked like my husband wasn't the slightest bit interested in what I had to say. But I knew he was listening.

I stood there smiling at the zip-locked golf balls and whispered, "I'll come back for you later." I laughed a little at the thought of Romeo changing his mind. I'm optimistic that way. Either way, I wanted to flush golf balls down a toilet. Preferably ours. I didn't want to resort to going to a gas station with a purse full of golf balls and get arrested for clogging up a public toilet. I could see the headlines now, "Breaking News! Local Car Lot Owner Arrested for Flushing Balls Down a Public Toilet."

With the help of a local plumber, police officers were able to convince a local business owner—with false promises of a new toilet—to abandon the gas station restroom. A straitjacket was used to restrain the suspect before putting her in the paddy wagon. Officers were baffled as to why the woman continued to scream her request over and over: "Let me flush my balls! Let me flush my balls!"

I had to flush golf balls for the curious consumers, the scientific wannabes and the flushing community. I needed to know if Sir Johnny could handle golf ball sized clogs. If it worked, Sir Johnny would have bragging rights. If it didn't work, I'd call a plumber before Romeo got home and he'd never know the difference. It was a win-win.

In any case, our bathroom remodel was underway, and I was permanently distracted from the craziness at the lot while it lingered on. Romeo, the love of my life, was indulging my needs, even if he was neglecting me in the area of flushing balls. I didn't think it would be long before he saw things my way.

Chapter Five

♡

SICK DAYS

Shortly after our remodeling project was underway, I woke up puking sick—so sick that I just wanted to crawl back into bed and be left alone. I was the type of person that said, "It'll go away." I usually waited too long before going to see a doctor, and that got on Romeo's nerves. I'd rather suffer and hope to get better than to go see a doctor, but I'd been getting worse during the previous week.

I hated going to see doctors because they gave me bad news that I already knew. Why bother to confirm it? Besides, it was my duty to try and save our insurance company some money in hopes that they'd lower our rates.

With Google's help, I was doing my part. I called it Googlecare.

Insurance companies should give discounts to people who rarely use their service. We pay up the ass for that coverage, so we should get rewarded when we don't use it. Reward points in the form of a cash refund would be nice.

Doctors wanted me to pay them just so they could tell me I was sick. I already knew I was sick, so I didn't need a doctor to tell me what I already knew. Seemed to me, if I accurately self-diagnosed without needing eight years of med school, then I should get some type of discount for figuring it out all by myself.

Or maybe doctors should start an incentive program. The insurance companies would love them and so would their patients. There's a huge part of the population who hate visiting the doctor. I don't want to give doctors a complex or anything, but people like me don't like to hear bad news. I don't have a doctor phobia or anything and I'm sure there's a word for that, but I was sick and didn't want to do a Google search. Doctors could get more people to come see them if after ten doctor visits, the patient gets one free. Give me a punch card, because that idea sounded good to me.

I loved my doctor. I was just a grouchy-ass bitch when I didn't feel good, and I didn't like taking medication because I was allergic to too many things.

I hated to admit it, but I was a defeated warrior. After too many times staring down Sir Johnny, it was past time for me to seek medical advice. I needed to go to the walk-in clinic because I couldn't get an appointment to see my regular family doctor. Why did I want to wait another day when I finally admitted that I could use some professional help? Besides, Google didn't prescribe antibiotics. I checked. It was hard enough to swallow my pride to make the call. If I waited another day, I could literally die. The flu was making its contagious rounds in our community and I was one of the lucky people to catch it. Yay, for me.

I went to the clinic and put on a surgical mask available at the door. I wasn't sure how much those little beauties helped protect against the spread of germs, but hey, it was free and the sign said to use one. I wrote my name on the clipboard, then took a seat and waited my turn. I dozed off several times and didn't care what other people thought of me. Honestly, if the chairs weren't separated with those stupid handles, I would've spread out and used my purse as a pillow. Screw dignity. I felt like shit and I didn't care.

It was a good thing I had my cell phone

with me because the waiting room didn't have a clock. I waited nearly an hour. They knew I was sick, because I told them when I signed in. All I wanted was to be home in my bed, not here among a bunch of sickly strangers. None of them looked as bad as I felt, nor was anyone else coughing up a lung. I should've been first in line.

Finally, it was my turn. To make me feel even shittier, I had to step on a scale. I didn't know why they wanted to know if I was losing weight or getting fatter since my last visit. I didn't understand why my height had to be measured either. I'm almost fifty years old and I stopped growing years ago. Maybe they thought I was a candidate for bone deterioration at my age or something. Again, another reason I didn't want to go to doctors, because they take notes on everything and might one day tell me I was getting shorter. I made a mental note to Google "shrinking diseases" when I felt better.

When called into the exam room, I plopped down in the chair. The exam table was too high for me to bother exerting any extra energy by stepping on the child stool to reach it. If I'd managed to get on that table, I'd have laid down and taken another nap. The nurse took my blood pressure and temperature, as usual, then asked a bunch of questions that were irrelevant to my situation.

I glanced around for a clock. Nope. There was no clock in this room either. I waited another forty-five minutes before the doctor knocked on my exam room door. Forty-five minutes! Apparently, the nurse forgot to tell the doctor that I was on my deathbed.

The doctor entered the room, greeted me with a tired smile, then asked me why I was there. It was all I could do not to roll my eyes. All he had to do was look at my chart and see the word "dying" on there. I didn't have to narrow my eyes because they were already part way there. I glared at the doctor and replied, "I'm sick."

That doctor wasn't going to give me any discount for my self-diagnosis via Google-care—no matter how reliable—so it was time he earned his money. My bitchy attitude was shining through that morning. No doubt my mom would've been appalled by my bad temper. It was probably a good thing she lived in another town.

The doctor finally told me I had the flu, which I already knew. Since I waited so long to go see a doctor in the first place, the flu medication wouldn't work now. I hated medicine anyway. To my surprise, the congestion made its way into my lungs. Now I had to worry about getting pneumonia on top of having the flu. Could my day get any worse?

I made sure to get a doctor's note. I had to give it to my boss, a.k.a. Romeo, so I didn't have to work. I did it so I could justify closing the office. I taped a sign on the office door that read: *Office closed due to illness. To prevent continued spread of the flu virus in our community, the office will be closed for the rest of the week.*

Living next door to our car lot had its advantages and disadvantages. That day demonstrated one of the disadvantages. The phone rang off the hook like a telethon. My guess was that sick people were magnets for phone calls and unexpected visitors.

The business line was forwarded to my cell phone and I didn't know how to stop it, nor did I feel like trying to figure it out. A certain phone number repeatedly called over and over and I refused to answer. I couldn't get any rest. Why couldn't the caller just leave a message like normal people did? I refused to answer. It was a fucking showdown. Maybe I should've turned my phone off or recorded a new message, but I sounded like shit and I was too sick to be bothered doing it.

An hour later, someone was ringing the buzzer at the office door, ignoring the sick sign taped to it. The buzzer was wired to ring in our home and that was how technology sometimes invaded my personal life. Foxy Boxy was going ape-shit crazy and barking her head off and making mine feel worse.

I dragged myself off the couch, then put my shoes and jacket on. By the time I got outside the guy was gone. So, I called the number. Sure enough it was the same guy who was ringing the buzzer. "Yeah, I just walked three miles to buy a car and you're not in the office."

I rolled my eyes since he couldn't see me. "That's because I'm sick with the flu. I put a sign on the office door. Didn't you see it?"

"Look," the customer said. "I'm not trying to be mean or anything, but in your line of work you need to be available for the customer during your working hours, regardless of being sick. I intend on buying a vehicle today and I expect you to be in your office. I'll be back in a few hours."

I gritted my teeth. "Fine."

He could clearly hear I was sick and didn't even care. Another resident of Stupidville was making himself known. I didn't get paid enough to deal with assholes like him. Damn, I didn't get paid at all. If the car lot didn't need the money, I might have told him what I really thought.

♡ ♡ ♡

Two hours later a familiar car pulled in the driveway. A man and a woman got out and I immediately recognized the woman. She was a very nice lady who had purchased a vehicle from us several years ago. I made a point to ignore the man. After all, he was the one that gave me attitude over the phone and forced me to be available to sell him a vehicle. Right away, the woman knew I was sick and felt bad for bringing her friend to the lot and apologized.

I had a coughing fit and covered my mouth with my hand. I had already tossed the white surgical mask in the trash. I made a mental note to email the surgical mask designers and request they offer them in pink. If it was pink, I might have considered wearing it longer or keeping it as a souvenir since the doctor didn't give me a sticker like the kids got.

The man walked over and stuck out his hand to shake mine. I smiled weakly and gladly shook his hand with the one I coughed on. I secretly hoped my germ-infested hand gave him the flu. My hope shattered when he said I should've gotten a flu shot like he did. It served me right for wishing ill on someone.

Next time I get sick, I will turn my phone off and unplug the buzzer. If that didn't work,

I would go to a hotel. I thought about buying some quarantine tape to hang on the office door, but with my luck, a customer might take a photo, then it would end up in the newspaper or all over the Internet. I totally needed to rethink this.

The man took the vehicle out for a test-drive and while he was gone, I rested my head on my desk, closed my eyes and tried to take a catnap. I hoped he would go home and think about it and come back another day. But that didn't happen. When he returned he indicated that he wanted to buy the car.

My head was pounding and I couldn't think straight. As a result, the paperwork, that should've taken less than an hour, actually took two hours to complete. The customer's bad attitude shifted and he became a well-mannered gentleman, along with "please" and "thank you."

He sat in the car staying warm while I scraped off the writing on the windows and attached the thirty-day temporary tag to the rear of the vehicle. I thanked him for the business, then said goodbye.

It was past time for me to get some much-needed rest. I went inside our home, locked the door, turned the lights off and put my phone on silent, then plopped down on the couch and fell fast asleep.

Foxy Boxy's barking woke me up when Romeo opened the door. I vaguely remembered Romeo touching my forehead and cheeks to check my temperature. "You're burning up," he hissed. A moment later he helped me to a sitting position and encouraged me to take some fever medication.

Romeo scooped up my phone, walked into the kitchen, checked the voicemail messages and returned all the missed calls. I heard him tell potential customers that the office would be closed the rest of the week.

God, I loved that man.

Chapter Six

DEALER AUCTION DAY

Thursday, the day hundreds of car dealers, in my area of the state, went to a dealer auction or attended the online sale. Dealers had to bid against each other to buy vehicles for their lots. It was a dealer-only auction, so the general public could not attend. Some days, I was lucky enough to outbid other dealers and go home with five or six vehicles.

Despite my attempts to downsize the lot, each new discovery on our bathroom project pushed it one layer deeper. The money had to come from somewhere. So when I was finally feeling better, I knew I had to make some bids. After kissing Romeo and sending him off to work, I had my own field trip to attend. Besides, any excuse to spend a day without customers was good enough for me.

To enter the dealer block—where the vehicles are paraded through a metal building consisting of ten lanes for buyer inspection—all dealers had to wear an assigned bidder badge, which is issued to them before they can bid. Most of the time, I was the only woman in attendance among an average of four hundred men. It was rare to see another female at the auctions because not many females owned or ran a car lot. I once counted a total of three women at the sale with dealer badges.

Among the swarms of dealers, cars rolled on and off the floor. I was careful not to step in front of any vehicles while they were moving, no matter how slow they plodded along. Sometimes they had bad brakes and have been known not to stop. On my way to get a better view of some newer cars, an Impala scooted dangerously close and smashed into the side of the building with a crunch. No one paid much attention—just another day at the auction.

Not only did I watch out for runaway vehicles or bad drivers, I kept a watchful eye out for certain dealers. Most of the dealers I knew were friendly, talkative and gave great advice. But some male dealers didn't think women should be allowed on the dealer block, even if they were a licensed dealer.

An hour into the sale, I spotted a sweet ride. It was retail red, and it caught my full attention. I made my way through the crowd of dealers and walked around it, checking for any dents, scratches or missing parts. All the while, I had my hand on the body of the car to feel for an engine or exhaust miss. At the rear of the vehicle, I observed the tailpipe and watched for smoke or dripping water to give me any indication of a blown head gasket. I then walked toward the hood of the vehicle, where another dealer had already opened it. I popped my head under the hood, to inspect the valve cover gaskets for any oil leaks and listened for any possible engine noises. A squeaky belt could easily be replaced, but a ticking engine would cost a lot of money to repair or replace. If I suspected major repairs needed to be done, I would only buy the vehicle if I could purchase it for a low price to accommodate for any repairs. Everything here looked great.

Satisfied with the purring engine, I walked to the driver side and leaned in to see if there were any warning lights lit up on the instrument cluster in the dash. Out of nowhere, a guy shoved me out of the way.

"Move!" he said. I stumbled sideways, but

thankfully I didn't fall. He didn't care.

"Fucking prick!" I retorted, but he ignored my comment. I then walked thirty feet to the front of the lane, so I could bid on the vehicle.

Each lane could easily hold three vehicles inside the building. Outside, four cars would be waiting in each line to enter through the bay doors. The dealer block was inside the building, where the actual bidding and buying took place. As one car was sold and pulled out of the building, the line would slowly move forward and another car entered. This parade of vehicles continued until all the lines were empty.

I spotted the guy who shoved me aside and watched him walk to the opposite side of the same lane. He wasn't the only dealer wanting that vehicle. I stepped to the edge of the white do-not-cross line so the auctioneer and floor guys could easily spot me when I placed a bid. At my height, if I stood behind other men, the auctioneer might not see me bid.

It was time for me to make a point. If that prick ended up being one of the higher bidders, I would either outbid him or drive the price up just to piss him off. I belonged here just as much as he did. I decided I might even overpay for the vehicle, or at least try to hurt that man's wallet. It would make me happy either way.

There were three cars in front of the vehicle I was waiting for, so I began listening to the auctioneer to get a feel for how he sold the cars. Each auctioneer had a different tactic. Some spoke slow enough to understand, while others spoke so fast it was possible two maybe three different languages were being used.

The next vehicle up for auction was a junky old beater. Smoke bellowed out of the loud exhaust system dragging on the ground. The hood, fenders and doors were all spray painted a different color. Although the car had a noticeable engine miss, at least it was running and didn't have to be pushed or hauled through the sale.

"Look what we have here, folks!" the auctioneer began. "It has a one of a kind paint job. No two dents are alike. I call that a work of art. Despite its unique appearance, the car report doesn't indicate any accidents in the history check. That means you get a clear title, folks! Can I get 500? Who will give me 500? 500. 500. 500." The auctioneer's chanting was nearly hypnotic. He hadn't got a single bid, so he broke his rhythm to speak to the crowd, again. "The twenty-inch rims are worth more than that, folks! You can sell them and junk the rest of the car. 500. Who will give me 500?

500. 500. 100 in the back! I got 100. Who will give me 200? 200. 200. 200."

Most dealer auctions have a system in place to run each vehicle identification number, as the car comes through the sale. The report disclosed anything in the vehicle's history that might give a buyer pause, like accidents, flood damage and odometer discrepancies. But sometimes I wondered if everything was actually reported. I was really curious about the creepier things. I wanted full disclosure.

For example, I wanted to know if a person had a heart attack and died in a car, or worse, died in a car from a drive-by shooting. As awful as that sounded, I'd bet good money it has happened.

I once watched a Cadillac go through a dealer auction I attended, all decked out with expensive twenty-inch rims, sunroof and leather interior. It was off-the-charts loaded. I glanced inside the car and noticed about twelve scattered holes in the leather of the backseat. Door panels and trim could easily be changed out, but replacing that expensive leather would have cost a mint. The seller just left it "as is," but the interior told the story.

Those bullet holes got me thinking that something might be missing from the vehicle reports. That Cadillac was probably haunted, like the car in Stephen King's novel, *Christine*. I had walked away from that vehicle—more like a light jog, really. I hadn't wanted any unfinished ghost business latching onto me and invading the car lot without an invitation. We certainly didn't want any mischievous ghosts causing problems, like grabbing the steering wheel while a potential customer was taking a test-drive. Our business insurance didn't cover paranormal activity. I checked.

The vehicle that Prick and I were watching pulled up and the bidding frenzy began. I waited patiently for the excitement to slow down, then caught the auctioneer's attention and raised my hand to place my first bid. After that, I would only give him a subtle nod of my head. Unless someone was specifically watching me, nobody knew I was one of the people bidding. Some men would drive the price of the vehicle up or purposely outbid me just because I was a woman. If I caught a dealer doing that to me, I would continue to bid to raise the cost, then step back and end my bidding. In the end, that dealer would be the one who overpaid, not me. Sometimes it backfired, but not often.

The auctioneer was interrupted by some loud dealer drama in the next lane. A bidding war had developed and a heated argument was in progress. The winning bidder was mad because he overpaid and the losing bidder was upset because he lost. I had my phone aimed at the dealers and tapped the record button. I hadn't witnessed a fistfight in a few months. Hot-tempers grew hotter and pushing turned into shoving. But the floor guys did their job and separated the two dealers before the first punch was thrown. Shit. I stopped the recording and turned back to refocus my attention on the car I wanted to buy.

The bidding was down to Prick and me. He didn't know I was the other bidder and kept looking around. At first he didn't believe the auctioneer had another bid and thought he was just driving up the price and tried to call him out on it.

"Who's the other bidder?" Prick challenged. But the auctioneer ignored him and kept chanting at an urgent pace.

Prick raised his hand to bid, then I would bid with another slight nod. All eyes were on Prick, and a few dealers looked around and tried to locate the hidden bidder. It went on and on. Still, nobody knew—except the auctioneer—that I was bidding against him. I held back my grin and kept sending the price up, up and up, until Prick shook his head, threw his hands in the air and stomped away. "Sold!"

The auctioneer yelled through the microphone and slammed his hand down. He then pointed at me, and in turn I pointed to my bidder badge.

"That'll teach you to fuck with me," I mumbled, then scouted another vehicle coming through the lanes.

It turned out Prick and I were both interested in the same vehicles. I continued to outbid him and purchased five vehicles. On car number six, I held the buyer sheets in my hand and made it known that I was bidding against him.

When the bidding began, Prick was the first to place a bid, then I held my hand up for the auctioneer and the surrounding dealers to see. That caught Prick's attention. Each time he bid, he would look at me to see if I would bid next. And I did. It went on and on. I drove the price up and grinned across the lane at Prick. His lips tightened into a thin line as he accepted defeat. After the auctioneer announced the car was sold, Prick stomped across the lane and came to a full stop directly in front of me.

"What are you trying to prove?" He pointed his finger inches away from my face.

I looked up at him and sneered, "If you ever lay a hand on me again, I'll put a restraining order against you. That means you'll never be able to attend a sale if I'm there. Do you understand?"

"You're a bitch!" He said, which caught the attention of the floor guy standing a few feet away from us.

"Everything okay, here?" The floor guy's voice boomed, aiming his question toward Prick.

I nodded my head with a grin. "Yes, everything is perfectly fine. This guy just told me that I was a Beautiful, Intelligent, Talented, Creative and Honest woman."

Prick huffed and puffed, but didn't blow the building down. He glanced between me and the floor guy, clenched his jaw, then spun on his heels and walked away.

Floor guy watched him go, then turned to me and said, "He called you a bitch. I heard it."

"Yeah," I giggled. "I wonder if he'll be here next week?"

♡ ♡ ♡

Late afternoon, I arrived back to our lot. Having bought three rather nice vehicles, I was on cloud nine. Although the office was officially closed on Thursday—so I could attend dealer auctions—I didn't mind helping people who came to the lot or called when I was finished.

After I parked, I went to check the mailbox, when another vehicle pulled into the lot. A woman dressed in casual clothes stepped out of her car and started looking around appearing to be undecided, going from one car to the next. I didn't bother most people when they were browsing, but my bladder was going to burst. An hour-long drive and a large drink had me squirming. The faster I helped her, the faster I could visit Sir Johnny.

As I approached the woman, she turned toward me. "Do you sell cars here?"

I was at a loss for words. There was no possible way I heard her correctly. We had a lot full of cars, a sign that clearly stated we sold cars, flags strung above the cars and an office sign too. We were obviously a car lot and we sold cars. Maybe I should wear a nametag.

I put my pinky finger in my ear, then wiggled it around a little. I even wondered if I could do a hearing test on Google. There had to be an app for that. If not, I could invent one and make millions of dollars. I made a mental note to do a search later.

"Excuse me?" I asked.

The woman folded her arms over her chest and asked again. "Do you sell cars here?"

I wondered if the insane asylum was missing a patient. I took a step back. Or maybe she just forgot to take her medication that morning. I could see the headlines, "Breaking News! Escaped Patient Found at Local Car Lot." The newspaper article would describe the scene as a business owner's nightmare.

Officers restrained a woman at a local car lot this afternoon with a straitjacket. As the paddy wagon left the lot, the woman continued to scream at the business owner, "Do you sell cars here?"

I pulled out my cell phone and tapped the screen to open the keypad just in case I had to call the police. I wasn't taking any chances. I thought about telling her that I sell possibilities to endless journeys and future memories, but I wanted to be a bit more sarcastic than that. I didn't think it could hurt the situation any.

"No." I said, "We sell stars. We have a large collection as you can see. Buy one, get one free. Keep one for yourself and give the other one away. It's totally up to you. You can even name it. But that's not even the best part. It comes with a verified certificate of authenticity and a 90-day warranty. Money back guaranteed. If you act now, I'll throw in a free balloon."

The woman grinned. "Are you Julia Karr?"

I took a step back and paused.

"That's me." This woman was starting to

freak me out. She then handed me a business card.

"I'm with the state inspectors office," She said. "I'm here to verify your dealer's license, business license and go over a few things with you."

Well, shit.

Of all the times for me be a smart-ass and play stupid, this shit happens. That would maybe teach me not to act like an idiot. Lesson learned.

I suppose I didn't make a good first impression.

She started going on and on about compliance statutes, regulations and fines, using words that even Google had to Google to find the definition of. My mind was reeling with every curse word I knew, but I bit my tongue.

Just to make sure, I briefly scanned all the cars to see if the necessary paperwork hung in each vehicle. If they weren't there, we'd get fined up the ass. We have never been fined because we had our shit together, but this surprise inspection made me nervous. And this inspector scared the crap out of me. I know some men would see a woman in power like her as just another crazy woman, clearly pre-menopausal, and out for blood (pun fully intended). For a brief moment, without defenses, I didn't blame them.

I got the feeling she was intentionally try-ing to intimidate me. She drummed on the glass of one of our cars, casually peering in, not talking to me. I knew we hadn't done any-thing wrong. Our dealer, business and sales licenses were hung prominently on the office wall. We kept records of all issued temporary tags and anything else she could possibly want to see or ask about. I had nothing to worry about, but I still didn't like surprise inspections or women with assertive attitudes. The saying "it takes one to know one," came to mind, but I brushed that thought away.

Imagine two aggressive Alpha Females with Type A personalities, both dealing with stupid on a daily basis, wanting to show our strength in the auto industry. No ninja-knife could cut through the tension in the air.

We went in the office to talk.

"We have some new regulations," she said. "I hope you're planning to comply."

I nearly rolled my eyes and wondered what she would say if I told her, "no."

She pushed a paper across the desk. The list seemed endless.

"Let's get this straight," I said. I read from the document. "'All forms must be taped inside the vehicle with at least three inches of clear glass on all sides.' So you want me to take a ruler to this?"

She smiled and nodded. She enjoyed making me squirm. So I continued to make her answer my absurd questions. I wasn't sure who actually won the bitch of the hour award, but I'd like to think it was a tie.

Eventually, the tension calmed down and I realized I liked her bold attitude. Then I found out she drove around all day, which would literally drive me insane. She visited hundreds of car dealerships in her assigned area of the state at least once per year. I bet handling an endless stream of dealers like my friend Prick from the auction would make for a tiresome day.

After finding out she didn't come to burst my ovaries, I tried to get to know her as a person instead of as an inspector. We were human—unless she was an alien, in which case I was probably on her most hated list.

"So do you like books?" She looked at me sadly.

"I'm way too tired to read when I get home." I'd probably feel the same way too, but I liked to encourage people to read.

I grabbed a copy of a thriller I'd finished the night before.

"It's a good one. Chaos and sarcasm fill these pages, and the detective woman kicks ass."

"Thanks," she said. I wasn't sure if she'd read it, but I knew I was doing my part to help a fellow badass woman out.

At the end of our first encounter, I realized that she had gifted me with the knowledge of new bullshit rules and regulations to incorporate into our business. But at the same time, I was happy to have met her. It was rare to meet another headstrong female.

It was too bad I didn't get the name of Prick's car lot because I would gladly ask her to visit him. I made a mental note to find out exactly who he was next Thursday.

Chapter Seven

♡

I'M ONLY HUMAN

I used to think Mondays were super crazy days that made everyone miserable. After some serious Google research following a particularly bad Monday morning, it turned out I wasn't crazy after all. Well, at least in regards to my thoughts on Mondays.

Searching for "Monday Statistics", a bunch of wacky shit came up. Monday is the day people were most likely to commit suicide or have a heart attack. Fifty percent of employees are late for work. Monday is also supposed to be the best day to buy a car.

Apparently, with weekend car sales being higher, many dealers are willing to make deals on Monday because the next weekend sales frenzy is almost a full week away. I was shocked to read that, but it all made sense. Even still, I wasn't jumping through hoops to sell cars on a Monday, because the weekend wore me the fuck out.

This particular Monday started out just like any other—some phone calls, title work, calling mechanics and answering emails. Then the shit hit the fan. It quickly turned up to some high-speed turbo blender setting.

With the invention of Bluetooth earbuds, my days of being tied to my office desk just to answer calls were a thing of the past. Since the office number was forwarded to my cell phone, I could take calls while making coffee, filling gas jugs, jumping cars with dead batteries, or filing paperwork. Hands-free multitasking was something I did well.

I hadn't put my air cast boot on yet, but I figured I had a few minutes before the lot got busy. I was so wrong. A car pulled onto the lot as soon as we opened and a nice young lady wanted to test-drive a vehicle. She had called over the weekend, but she couldn't get to our lot until this morning. After returning from her test-drive, she explained how much she loved it and filled out the necessary paperwork to put the vehicle on layaway.

Romeo came up with the layaway program idea about six years ago. At the end of 90 days, the customer came and filled out the paperwork, then drove off the lot with only a monthly payment-kudos to Romeo for having that light bulb of an idea. One tax season we had ten vehicles on layaway because people were waiting on their tax refunds and didn't want someone else coming along and buying the car they wanted. It worked out great, so we decided to keep it going year-round.

As soon as the young lady left the lot, I started toward our house to put my boot on and drink some coffee. The coffee was the perfect temperature and it tasted wonderful. I only got one tiny sip of heaven in before the phone rang.

"Cars To Go, Julia Karr speaking. How can I help you?" I lifted the cup of coffee to my lips to take another sip while I waited for a reply.

"Hello," a man said over the phone. "I met Stella at a bar last night and she said she ran this car lot. She said she'd give me a good deal."

I started choking on the coffee and spitting it everywhere. "I'm sorry. You must have the wrong number. I don't know any Stella. Only my husband and I run this car lot. And I wasn't at a bar last night."

"Okay. Sorry," the man said, then hung up.

While I watched the video monitors, I grabbed a sponge and started soaking up the coffee I had just splattered everywhere. Then I noticed another vehicle pulling onto the lot. I rushed out the door before Foxy Boxy went crazy from the sound of the doorbell. I chided myself for not taking a moment to put my boot on instead of nursing my coffee, but I wasn't too worried about it. It's not like Romeo or my doctor would find out, and it would only take a moment to put it on after I finished helping this customer.

When I got to the office, the customer was waiting. He had come by the week before and was interested in a truck that we sent out to the mechanic to get new spark plugs and coil packs. On his earlier visit, I told him I'd hold the truck for him until we got it back to the lot. I promised I'd call him first before selling it to anyone else, so he was checking in to see how it was doing. The truck was ready, but we hadn't gone down to pick it up yet.

He offered to go with me to our mechanic's shop, which was only a quarter mile down the road, to test-drive it and return it to our lot. I closed the office, drove the customer to the truck and, after he left for his test-drive, I went back inside to pay the bill.

As I turned to leave the counter, I heard a

voice in the lobby say, "Hello, Julia." I saw a man who I'd sold a car to four years earlier waiting in the lobby. I smiled and returned his salutations with a kind "Hello."

The lobby was full of people, who were patiently waiting for oil changes, tire changes, and other repairs. Apparently, they were bored and didn't mind listening in on other people's conversations. I totally get that, because some conversations could be amusing, but I didn't suspect ours would amount to anything except the casual *hello and goodbye.*

"You remember the car you sold me?" the man asked.

"Yeah. It was a nice car," I replied, not sure where he was going with this. Maybe he sold it and was in the market to buy another vehicle. That happened sometimes when I saw former customers in public places.

"It's a piece of junk!"

I didn't expect to hear that. But this was the same guy who called me, after buying the vehicle, and asked if the car used gas or diesel fuel. The same guy who called me two days later and asked if we were going to buy him some new floor mats, because his car didn't come with any. The same guy who came to the office to make a payment and out of nowhere told me his wife used sex toys, because he couldn't get an erection. I was curious enough to play along.

"Really? What's wrong with it?" I inquired.

Junk Guy folded his arms across his chest. "A year after I bought it, I had to buy a new battery. And now it needs a starter."

This was the type of customer who thought he could call me out in front of a bunch of strangers and embarrass me. He was hoping to rattle me enough to get our business to pay for his starter. Stupid man. All he managed to do was piss me off like he did with the sex toy comment. I thought I'd teach him a valuable lesson and maybe shame him a little for trying to give our business a bad name in front of a bunch of people.

I pulled my shoulders back, turned my body toward him and looked him in the eye.

"You call that junk?" I said. "You've owned it for four years and that's all you've had to do to it? Holy cheese balls." I threw my hands in the air. "I wish that was all I had to do to my vehicle in the past four years."

A man sitting next to him interrupted and said, "Yeah. Me too."

Junk Guy's face began to flush a shade of red and he stumbled on his words. "I... I didn't mean it that way."

"What did you mean, then?" I challenged,

but he didn't respond.

A few of the people in the lobby started giggling and few others coughed to cover up their laughter. A young boy asked his mom if he could have some cheese balls. Yep, they were totally listening. I rolled my eyes at the guy and exited the lobby with my cheese ball attitude in tow.

When I got back to the lot, I changed the office door sign from closed to open. I didn't get twenty-five feet toward the house before my customer pulled back on the lot with the truck from the mechanic. He got out and shook his head.

"What's wrong?" I asked.

He explained that the engine still had a misfire with the spark plugs. After we talked, he was kind enough to drive the truck back to the mechanic for me. I hopped back in my vehicle so I could pick him up and hear what the mechanic had to say. It had to be something simple. Sometimes new parts were defective.

I tried my best to put the customer at ease. He wanted the truck, but after test-driving it twice, he was reluctant to buy it. I understood his reasoning and I went on to explain that I wouldn't sell the truck until it was fixed properly. The customer might not have known how we did business, but I made sure he knew we were honest and upfront about every vehicle we sold.

I brought him back to the lot, and I felt bad that someone was hesitant to buy a vehicle from us. Nevertheless, the truck would sell. Maybe not to him, but someone would want to buy it because it was a nice truck. The customer walked to his car and I headed toward my house. The wind was blowing something fierce and it was beginning to rain. He said something, which made me turn around and I saw him hold his hand up like he was waving. I assumed he was saying goodbye and I said goodbye too. I wasn't even sure he heard me over the wind because I didn't actually hear him say goodbye either.

The phone was ringing by the time I got inside the house, so I answered it.

"I know this is the car lot where Stella works," the male voice said. "She told me she ran the place and would give me a good deal. I need to talk to her."

"For the love of God," I mumbled, not caring if he heard me. "Look. We don't have any employees. Stella lied to you. She doesn't work here."

"Okay, sorry," the man said, then hung up.

I managed to put my air cast on just as

another customer pulled onto the lot. He was looking for a truck for his son. He test-drove two, then inquired about the truck at the mechanic's shop just down the road. In a small town like this, some people stalked our website, watched our lot, and knew the inventory.

I explained what had happened with the truck, and he was still interested. Then he asked if I could let him know when it was ready for a test-drive. I was writing down his number as a nice young couple walked into the office.

I made a mental note to do a Google search about "love your truck day."

The couple had overheard us and asked about the truck at the mechanic. It was nearly closing time, so I decided to call the mechanic and let him know I had someone else interested in the truck, too. I explained the situation to them and they wanted to wait to see if the mechanic called me back.

Ten minutes later, the mechanic called me back and said one of the new coil packs was defective and that the parts store replaced it with another one. The couple agreed to go to the mechanic and test-drive the truck from there and bring it back to our lot afterwards.

I had a few minutes to grab a quick bite to eat while they were gone. I barely managed to get a few sips of coffee this morning before truck day started in earnest, and it was all I managed to get all day. I opened a small bag of chips and devoured them like a wild animal. It was a good thing nobody was around to judge me and my eating habits, but at that point I wouldn't have cared anyway.

After returning from the test-drive, the couple immediately put some money down to hold the truck on layaway. I didn't know what was so special about that truck, but damn. I needed to buy twenty more of them.

While I was filling out the layaway agreement, the phone started ringing. I answered the call and continued to fill out the paperwork. "Cars to Go. How can I help you?"

On the other end of the line, a man cleared his throat. "Can I speak to Stella? I met her at a bar last night."

This man was getting on my last nerve. I dropped my pen on the desk, then spun my chair around so I faced the wall and lowered my voice. "Listen up dude. My guess is that this Stella was pulling your leg or you misunderstood what car lot she worked at."

"Would you give me a good deal?" the man asked.

I wasn't sure what type of good deal the mystery woman promised the man, but I wasn't taking any chances. "No. I'm not Stella. If you call again, I'll call the police."

"Okay, okay. Sorry," he said, then hung up.

While the couple was signing the layaway agreement the gentleman who originally test-drove the truck and was reluctant to buy it sent me a text message. My cell phone number was on our business cards and I occasionally received text messages from various customers, so it wasn't unusual. He asked if I had heard anything from the mechanic about the truck.

What the hell? The last thing I remembered him saying about that truck was that he was reluctant to buy it. I replied to the text and said someone test-drove it and put it on layaway. I also explained what the problem was with the coil pack. I figured he was just curious and that was the end of it.

During dinner I told Romeo about the mysterious caller.

"He kept insisting on finding Stella." Romeo just shook his head and laughed.

"I know Stella," he said. "Back from before I met you, an old flame. I bet she still has one of the business cards I handed out at my class reunion. Probably uses it to chase away creepy dudes." Romeo laughed again.

I busted out laughing too because I had

done something similar back when I was dat-ing. A guy once asked for my phone number and I gave him the number to a local pizza joint. I had certain phone numbers memorized because I didn't want to look them up in the phonebook or call the operator for assistance.

An hour later, I received a reply to the text message I sent earlier to the guy who I thought didn't want the truck.

Customer: You sold it?
Me: Yes, someone put it on layaway.
Customer: I thought you said it was mine. You would hold it for me. We had a deal.

I started to reply, but before I could finish typing the customer called me. He wasn't happy. Neither was I for that matter. One, I don't answer business calls after hours, but if I didn't take his call, I'd look like a bitch. Two, he said he was reluctant to buy the truck. Three, my foot was killing me. I only had the boot on for three hours instead of all day like the doctor recommended.

By the time I got off the phone, I felt like a shitty person. I thought of the proverbial crooked car dealer wanting to sell a vehicle to the first person that came along. I didn't do anything wrong, but the customer made me feel like I did. It bothered me because I have a conscience. The almost-customer was polite in a forceful kind of way. I defended what I thought he had said. Apparently, when I *assumed* he was saying goodbye during the crazy wind and rain, he had actually told me to text him when the truck was ready. But I didn't hear him. The last thing I knew was that he didn't want the truck.

I didn't sleep well that night.

The next morning, I sent the customer another text. I could've left things alone and let him bad-mouth me and our business—not that he would've done that, but I didn't like the idea that he might. I wasn't the type of dealer who would sell a car out from under someone just to make a dollar. That would be wrong. I was an honest person, and proud of it.

Me: I just want to say I'm sorry for my mistake. In 15 years, I've not made a mistake like that. My apologies. Please, forgive me. Have a wonderful week.

Customer: LOL it's fine. God only made one perfect person. I should have made myself clearer.

Me: I had to text you because it bothered me all night. I've never made a mistake like that. Thank you for understanding.

Customer: Like I said, it's fine and thank you for taking the time to text me.

At that point, I felt a little better, but I wasn't sure if I had made a new future customer or lost one. Time would only tell. Or maybe the guy looking for Stella would buy a car and balance everything out.

Chapter Eight

REPO THIEF

The next morning the phone rang several times before we opened, but I refused to answer it. I just wanted to complete some paperwork and finish drinking my coffee without interruption. At exactly ten A.M. the phone rang again.

"Cars to go. This is Julia. How can I help you?"

"Do you offer rewards for vehicles you're looking for?" A woman inquired.

"You mean vehicles in repossession status?" I asked.

"Yes," she eagerly replied.

"Yes, we do. And the repo agent won't mention how he found the car either." I held my breath and hoped the caller would give us a lead on a missing car in repo status.

"Okay, great!" The woman shouted down the phone. "I know the location of one of your cars. The person who has it is a family member and was bragging about hiding it from you. It's just not right." The customer gave me the information about the location of the car. She was happy to know that her relative would never know that she was the person who helped us. The finder's fee was just an added bonus.

"Thank you so much for all your help. I'll call you back after the repo agent locates the vehicle." I hung up, then called Tiny and gave him the updated information.

Tiny was the guy I called, when we had to order a repo. There was nothing tiny about Tiny. He was a big man, with an even bigger attitude. He drove a big truck and carried a big gun. Tiny was kindhearted and well man- nered, but he didn't take shit from anyone.

As soon as I hung up the phone, I knew my mood would be touch-and-go for the rest of the day and I didn't like it. I never knew how a person would react to the shame or embar- rassment of losing their vehicle. I've watched repo shows on television, and later learned that some were fabricated for ratings, but they still worried me just the same. I've never ordered a repo and had a customer go all ape-shit crazy, but it was best to stay on alert just in case.

I've heard stories about some dealers who enjoyed ordering repos just so they are able to turn around and sell the car again, thus making more money off the same vehicle. We weren't that way. We tried our best to work with our customers and went out of our way to help them.

When customers fell behind on their payments and the car was in repossession status, I did everything I could to get in touch with the customer and avoid ordering a repo. I made calls, mailed letters, sent emails and text messages. Sadly, when I was ignored, I had no choice but to order a repo.

It was often only when a repo car arrived at the lot that the customer who lost their vehicle would start calling and leaving me messages. I wondered why they hadn't contacted me to avoid the repo in the first place. When they called they'd demand that I call them back. I'd return the call, but I wasn't given the same courtesy when I politely asked them to call me in order to prevent it from happening in the first place. At least I was polite about it.

Some customers were friendly; they knew they couldn't afford the vehicle. When they had no means to bring their accounts current, most of them were kind about the entire situation and even returned the vehicle to the lot. When those particular customers got back on their feet, we'd help them get into another vehicle. Sometimes, unexpected things happened and we understood.

However, there were those few customers that would shock the shit out of me. And that's just what happened that morning.

When Tiny located the vehicle, the mysterious family member called about, he returned it to the lot. I had every intention of moving it to a secure location, but I had an urgent appointment with our toilet. I had already called our local police department and faxed them the repossession affidavit to let them know we currently had the vehicle in our possession. It was one of our local law enforcement rules, just in case a customer tried to report the car stolen. It made a lot of sense.

I only needed a few minutes with Sir Johnny to relieve my bladder. While I was putting my jacket back on, I heard a vehicle start. I looked at the video monitors, but I didn't see anything out of place or anyone walking around on the lot. Then I noticed a car moving.

The repo car was in reverse and slowly backing out of the parking spot just past the office

door. I freaked out and flew out the door.
Nobody was going to steal from us. Nobody.
I didn't have my gun on me, but that wasn't
going to prevent me from stopping a dirty
thief.

I could see the customer who fell behind
on his payments and refused to respond to my
calls behind the wheel of the car attempting to
steal it back. What the hell?

The car was moving in reverse when I
opened the passenger side door and jumped in
with one knee landing on the passenger seat.
The guy was shocked at my actions and to be
honest, so was I. In response, he put his foot on
the brake to stop the car. I put my hand on the
center gearshift to move it up into park, but
that dumb-ass started bashing my hand away.
The pain and bruising would come later, but
in that moment, I didn't give a shit. I was a
ninja warrior.

I lunged toward the ignition to remove the
key but again he punched my hand away. I
moved my hand from the ignition to the gearshift. As he batted my hand from the gearshift,
I moved my hand back to the ignition. Back
and forth, over and over. My hand was beginning to hurt. My feeble attempts to stop him
from taking the car looked slim, but then I
stopped and just looked at him. Our faces were

inches apart and his expression told me everything. That lunatic was trying to decide if he was going to hurt me or let the car go.

I never saw that look on anyone's face in my life and I would never forget it. All of a sudden, a sense of calm washed over Carjacker's face and he raised both of his hands in the air to surrender. "Okay. Okay," he said. "You're fucking nuts, lady."

My inner ninja almost laughed at that comment. Instead, I lowered my voice and said, "Yes, I am."

How someone could go from crazy to placid in an instant was unforgettable. I didn't hesitate. In a flash I shoved the gearshift into park, removed the key and stepped out of the car before he changed his mind.

I stood about ten feet away on the passenger side of the car and called the police. Meanwhile, Carjacker had got out of the car and was pacing around, mumbling shit.

"I just wanted to get my stuff out of the car."

I held up a hand to signal him to shut up. He couldn't be serious. There were better ways to get his things than stealing a car.

He produced a plastic grocery bag from the back seat and searched the entire car, including the trunk. He only filled the bag halfway. In other words, there wasn't much he'd left in the car. As he was doing this, I called my friend Ginger, who said she'd be right over.

Ginger was also a small business owner. She managed the local *Get the Funk Out Laundromat*. It was located between the *Amigone Funeral Home* and an old oil change building that was recently converted to *Jack the Clipper Barbershop*.

When Carjacker was finished, he took off walking with the bag slung over his shoulder.

About one minute after Carjacker left, the police arrived. My hands were shaking and tears welled up in my eyes. I felt like throwing up and I was angry with myself. The situation could've gotten out of control and far beyond what my imagination wanted me to admit.

Ginger arrived shortly after the police did. I answered the officer's questions and described Carjacker. Ginger overheard the description and said she had passed the guy walking not far from the lot. I gave a copy of his driver's license to the police officer, then he left to take care of the situation.

Meanwhile, more customers arrived wanting to test-drive vehicles. Ginger stood guard and basically interviewed everyone that walked into the office. She interrogated them just like a father questioned a new boy wanting to date his daughter. To the new potential customers, it was a typical day, nothing out of the ordinary.

After test-driving a few vehicles, one nice couple was ready to purchase a car and I guided them into the office to start the paperwork. I pasted on a smile and tried to make small talk, but they noticed my hands shaking and asked me if I was okay.

I told them the story, which put the man on edge. Throughout the entire process of purchasing the vehicle, he watched the lot through the large window and made a point to tell me about every person looking around on the lot, as if there was cause for concern that Carjacker would strike again.

"A car just pulled on the lot," he said.

I glanced out the window. "They're probably scoping out the place."

"Someone else is here," he said, then pointed out the window. "Do you know them?"

I glanced out the window again. "No, but he looks like an alien." My mind was making my mouth say stupid shit in order to distract me from the incident.

He ignored my response. "What was the guy wearing?"

"A pink bikini," I said, not looking up from the paperwork. "And in my opinion, it wasn't his color."

He leaned forward. "You can't be serious?"

"I never am."

The customer laughed so hard it brought tears to his eyes. It was just the funny moment I needed to help me calm down, but I understood what he was doing. He was a man and his protective instinct had kicked in—not only for his wife, but for me, as well. As long as he was in the office, he would make sure no harm came to any of us. Deep inside, past my fake smiles and silly comments, I needed that reassurance after what had happened.

When the sale was complete, I closed the lot and sent a text message to Romeo explaining a little about what had happened. I'd explain the entire episode with more details to him later. I left, then went to Ginger's laundromat and helped her fold laundry, while I waited for Romeo to get off work.

I knew the moment Romeo arrived home because I was watching the lot through the video cameras on my snazzy smartphone. He moved the repo car to a more secure location, walked around the lot, checked a few things, then sent me a text to let me know he was home.

I was worried Romeo was going to give me a long lecture, or worse, yell at me. I knew I had done something stupid. I put my life in danger to prevent an idiot from stealing a car. A vehicle could be replaced, but not my life. The man could've easily gone to jail for grand theft auto if I hadn't done anything. None of those things entered my mind at the time. It was only afterward that I started chiding myself for being so stupid. I felt like a defeated ninja warrior, even though I didn't let the bad guy get away.

Romeo leaned against the kitchen counter with his arms crossed over his chest, while I paced the floor and explained the entire episode. We watched the video and saw Carjacker's bad intentions. He peeked around the corner of the building a few times before he dashed for the vehicle, jerked the door open and attempted to leave. Romeo placed both hands on the counter and leaned closer to the monitor when badass ninja made her appearance and did her thing.

Watching the entire scene unfold before my eyes, rehashing it visually just freaked me out even more. I knew Romeo was stunned because it was a while before he spoke. When he did, he leaned against the kitchen counter again with his arms crossed over his chest. I could tell he was trying to remain calm for my benefit. But I could also tell he wanted to ring my neck.

"You might not think this is funny now," he said. "But you will in the future."

I looked at him with sad puppy eyes. "What?"

"I'm the only person in this house allowed to do crazy shit like that. Understand?" He raised an eyebrow and waited for my answer.

Whew, that was close. I thought he was going to lecture me or yell or something. "I'll let you know when I do," I said. He then pulled me close, wrapped his loving arms around me and gave me a big hug. That Romeo, he's a keeper.

On the lighter side of things, when we reviewed the video again, it very clearly showed a badass Hobbit-sized ninja warrior— me—without thy sword hammer. It looked like I was going to kick that man's ass. I was awesome.

But soon after my reprieve from scolding, I started to realize exactly what I had done and my mind started to slowly shut down. I was proud that I didn't back down, but I didn't want to think about it anymore. I wanted to go hide like a scared kid or drink some wine to forget about it. I wanted to call my parents and tell them what happened, but I didn't want them to worry, too. No, I had to be a brave little ninja.

Later that evening, Romeo wanted to take

me out to dinner. I was all for it at first, but I was also reluctant to leave our home. I wanted to leave and get away from this place, to hide, to feel safe. But on the other hand, I wanted to stay and protect our home. It took me about 30 minutes, but I finally agreed and we went out to dinner. The entire time we were gone, my mind was temporarily screwed up. The pain and bruising on my hand and wrist were a constant reminder of what had happened. I was reluctant to go home, yet I wanted to be sure everything was safe.

I didn't get much sleep that night, but someone had to do guard duty. I didn't go to bed until daybreak. At least I managed to get a few hours of sleep before I had to open the car lot.

During those sleepless hours, I used an ice pack on my hand and wrist and reached out to Google for answers concerning the after effects of fight or flight. I had all the typical side effects, but what I found interesting was the reasons why I didn't feel the pain in my hand until long after the incident. Apparently, my perception of pain was diminished by my body's natural painkiller, the endorphins that surged through this ninja warrior. That was so cool.

The next morning I was sleepless and still on

edge. I realized I forgot to call the anonymous family member back to give her the reward money. I called her that afternoon and told her what had happened. She apologized for what her call put into motion, but she didn't seem to be surprised by the outcome. She gave me her mailing address to send her a check, because she didn't want to be seen at the car lot.

Chapter Nine

SAME SHIT, DIFFERENT TOILET

The next Evil Monday started without any complications. I woke up early, drank a full cup of coffee, finished some office work and started on a few other things. I was beginning to think I should rename Evil Monday to Normal Monday. I couldn't remember the last time I had a great Monday. That was how rare they were.

I think the government should conduct a study about Evil Mondays to find out just how many people actually had great Mondays. Made perfect sense to me. Then maybe the new normal would be a three-day weekend instead of the current two days. The government wouldn't listen to me, same as the cereal and jean companies didn't. Neither would the leg cast designers, medical supply companies, doctors or insurance companies. I made a mental note to Google my own online study.

I finished doing the title transfers at the County Clerk's office and headed toward my pink Volkswagen Beetle. After making my way through the rows of vehicles, I found two ladies taking photos of my Bug. When I bought my Beetle, I felt it deserved a name, and Holly came to mind. Then I had the bright idea of buying Beetle eyelids and adding 3-D eyelashes to connect to the pink eyelids. Holly was kind of awesome. She drew a lot of attention and people loved taking photos of her.

I left the County Clerk's office and headed back to the lot. Romeo called me on his lunch break. "Hello you sexy thing," I said in a sultry voice. I couldn't help but giggle. I enjoyed catching Romeo off guard.

"Sexy huh?" Romeo chuckled, "Busy day?"

"Not really," I replied. "I just left the clerk's office with the title transfers and I'm going back to the lot."

"Good day then?" Romeo was shocked.

"Yeah, so far," I said. "Boring, but good."

About a mile down the road, when the traffic began to slow, I glanced over at a gas station and saw a car we had ordered for repossession a month ago. Tiny hadn't been able to locate it. We assumed the customer had moved or left the state because none of his references claimed to know his whereabouts. It was either that or they refused to tell us, which was probably the case.

"There's that bastard!" I yelled to myself when I saw the car.

"Who?" Romeo asked still listening to my real-world encounter.

I had no time to talk. I simply said, "I'll call you back." Without another thought, I hung up the phone, whipped Holly into the gas station and pulled behind that bastard's car to block him in. I got out and slammed the door. That got the attention of just about everyone there. The initial look on the customer's face made me want to laugh.

The man was at least six-foot tall and I wasn't even close. He was a big man, not obese, just big as God intended him to be. The image of a football player came to mind, but I had no intention of backing away. My adrenaline made me feel like a badass five-foot two-inch ninja warrior and I was going to take this fucker down or call the police. There was no time to call the Tiny. I had to do this myself. I had to be brave and channel my inner ninja warrior. I walked right up to him, stood two arms lengths away and raised my chin. Badass ninja warrior had taken over my entire being. Adrenaline pumped through my body and my pulse raced like Speedy Gonzalez. I was unstoppable. "Give me the payments or your car key, now," I demanded, then held out my hand for either of the two.

"Oh, yeah?" The guy challenged me.

"Yeah." I locked eyes with him. I wasn't going anywhere. It was like David and Goliath. The small crowd gathered around the food vender, paying attention to our raised voices. They were probably taking bets. I should've gotten in on a piece of that action because the odds were lopsided and I knew who would win.

Goliath took a step back, gave an assuring glance to the gathering crowd, then laughed a little. His cheeks betrayed him by flushing a shade pink in embarrassment. My attitude didn't waver. I was one badass chick.

"I've got all day," I said, then tapped my foot a few times. "Or I can call the police. Your choice." I felt I should give him an option so he thought he actually had one.

It was a showdown without the guns. Well, Goliath might have had a gun, I wasn't sure, but I didn't have mine. I gave him a cocky grin, crossed my arms over my chest and stood my ground. I didn't mind waiting. I wasn't moving and neither was my badass ninja Beetle. Basically, he was fucked. I thought there was no way Goliath had the money on him and if he decided to leave on foot without giving me the key, I'd just call a tow truck. No big deal. One way or another, I was going to get either the money or the car. I had already won and he didn't know it.

Goliath took out his wallet and handed me several 100-dollar bills. His wallet was stuffed with them. I didn't even have that much money in my personal bank account and I certainly wouldn't carry that kind of cash around with me, if I did.

It looked like a drug deal going down, but I didn't give a shit. I wasn't sure what he did to make all that money, but as long as I got what was owed to us, I didn't care. I folded the bills and tucked them into my front pocket, hoping they weren't counterfeit.

"If you want a receipt, you can come to the lot and get it," I said.

I didn't even thank him. I got into Holly, revved up the turbo-engine so the exhaust system screamed badass Beetle power, and squealed tires out of the parking lot. As soon as I got on the road, I called Romeo. He was probably worried or pissed off—maybe both—

because I didn't tell him what was going on. After Carjacker attempted to steal his car back, we were both on edge about repos. But I had no choice but to do what I did. Romeo would understand. Maybe not today, but he'd understand at some point, even if he didn't tell me.

"What the hell is going on?" Romeo demanded.

"There was a repo car. I blocked his ass in. You should've seen me. I was one badass bitch!" I yelled with excitement.

"You should've told me!" Romeo yelled back.

"Told you what? I didn't have time."

"Julia Karr, do you not understand why I'm upset?"

"Badass ninja bitch had it under control," I said with a little too much excitement. "I was awesome."

"We'll talk about this later." Then he hung up the phone.

Shit! Romeo might have been just a little bit pissed. Being a badass ninja bitch could've gotten me hurt or worse. It was a good thing the ninja in me didn't come out often.

Romeo would calm down before he got home. I was almost sure of it. I'd cook lasagna and have a ten-dollar bottle of wine ready just in case.

About ten minutes after I got to the lot, Goliath arrived to get his receipt. That's twice he shocked me. He gave me some bullshit story about moving and having a new job. He didn't have time to call me. Apparently it was a coincidence when I caught up with him, because he was actually on his way to our office to pay and bring his account current.

"In three months, you couldn't find the time to call me?" I inquired.

"No, I was busy," Goliath said, then shrugged.

"For three months?"

"You know how it is." Then he opened his arms to act all innocent.

"No, I don't know how it is."

Goliath gave me his new address and cell phone number, and I updated the information in the computer system. When the customer left, I took a lunch break, so I could calm down. I seriously needed some wine. Corporate executives have a few drinks during their lunch hours; at least they do on television. But I couldn't bring myself to take a sip. If this day continued on its evil path, I'd have a glass of wine at closing time. Maybe three.

After my lunch break was over a woman came to the lot and wanted to test-drive a car. I always told people about any work we had a mechanic do to a vehicle. Full disclosure. I told her the car had new tires and brakes and she was glad to hear it. After giving her the key, I returned to the paperwork at my desk.

Sitting at my desk while responding to a few emails, I heard a crash and felt the building shake. Looking out the showroom window I noticed the woman had hit the concrete steps with the vehicle she was test-driving. I bolted out the door. The woman was standing on the other side of the car, holding the key.

"What happened?"

"I'm going to say it was faulty brakes," she said, then grinned. "I didn't like the car anyway." She tossed me the key over the car, turned and walked away.

I reached into my pocket to pull my cell phone out, so I could take a photo of her license plate, but it wasn't there. It was on my desk in the office. Shit!

"Where the hell are you going?" I yelled.

"I'm leaving." I heard her laugh as she got into her vehicle.

If I stopped Concrete Crasher, like I wanted to, I would end up in jail, and then the entire incident would appear in the newspaper. It was a good thing I had some self-control because I wanted to tackle her like a linebacker.

By the time I got to my phone, Concrete

Crasher had already left the lot. I didn't copy her driver's license or have her sign the test-drive sheet. I had nothing for the police and no proof of why she was driving the car. My blood pressure rose and my face began to warm. I wasn't even sure wine could help in this situation.

I had to wonder for a moment if Crasher knew the customer I had just embarrassed at the gas station. It was possible he asked her to test-drive a car and damage it on purpose. Stranger things have happened. I shook those thoughts out of my mind.

My day went from bad to worse. We were going to have to get the bumper repaired. My anger turned into a frenzy. I started making copies of the test-drive sheet and placed them on a clipboard next to the office door. Then I went to Walmart and purchased a second printer to place near the door, specifically for copying driver's licenses. From that point forward, no car would leave this lot unless the form was filled out and we had a copy of a driver's license.

Sometimes stupid customers, as well as my own mistakes, forced us to change the way we did business. It might take a little extra time and add additional paperwork, but it only took one bad apple to ruin "fast and easy" for everyone else.

I dreaded having to explain to Romeo that someone got away with damaging a vehicle. Instead, I started chanting happy things out loud: "Sell the car lot. Take a vacation. Drink wine. Sell. Vacation. Wine." It didn't help.

I wanted to hit something, like Crasher did, to get rid of some of my anger. I made my way toward the garage and started rummaging through tools and garden-ware. I lucked out and found an old rusted golf club and snatched up a few of Foxy Boxy's squeaky tennis balls.

When Romeo arrived home, I was swinging the golf club like a baseball bat and trying to hit the tennis ball toward the garage door. Out of the corner of my eye I could see him leaning against his truck watching me.

"I can't figure out if you're trying to play baseball, tennis or golf." I heard him chuckle, but ignored it because I was trying to concentrate. I took another swing at the tennis ball and missed.

"Playing golf is hard," I said.

Romeo pushed away from his truck and took a few steps forward. "Have you ever played golf?"

"No." I took another swing at the ball and clipped it just enough to make it fly above my head. At least I was making progress.

"Then how do you know it's hard?" Romeo asked, catching the fly ball with one hand.

I plucked the ball out of Romeo's hand and shook it in the air. "If I can't hit a tennis ball with a golf club, then I won't be able to hit a golf ball with it either."

Romeo laughed. "Somehow your reasoning makes sense."

I took another swing at the ball and missed, again. With my lack of skills, it was time I gave up on my baseball, tennis or golf dreams. I slung the golf club over my shoulder, picked up the tennis ball, and walked toward the house.

"Bad day, huh?" Romeo inquired and I nodded as he held open the door. "What do you do when life gives you lemons?" Romeo asked in a cheerful voice.

"Well," I began. "I heard that saying when I was a little girl and I've had a long time to think about it." I tossed the tennis ball and Foxy Boxy took off like a speed demon to catch it.

"And?" Romeo said and patiently waited for my reply.

"I'd find those stupid lemon trees and shake the hell out of them until they had no more lemons. And Google Maps could help me locate more of them!" My mind whirled with ideas and I turned toward Romeo. "If Google maps could pinpoint every fruit tree on the planet, then it could locate every vegetable garden, too."

"Julia," Romeo said. "What are you talking about?"

I rushed to the computer. "I just solved world hunger! I need to send Google an email."

Romeo leaned against the counter and pinched his nose, "You lost me."

"The government could make it mandatory that every city maintain a free food park with vegetables and fruit trees. Volunteers and people doing community service could maintain it for free. We should totally replace our front yard with a vegetable garden for people who need food. It's time we did our part. And maybe we'd get a tax break too."

As I was typing an email to Google, Romeo wrapped his arms around my waist and kissed the side of my cheek. "It must have been a really bad day. I'll order pizza."

God, I love that man. He totally got me.

Chapter Ten

RUNAWAY VAN

Our entire car lot wasn't level. Most of it was, but one area had a slight incline before it leveled out again. One morning a van pulled up and parked in one of the customer parking spots near the office door where the incline started to level out. Then a woman came inside with a young child. She liked her van but wanted to upgrade to a sports utility vehicle. When our kids were small, we owned a minivan too, but those old school vans didn't have all the options that made a family-friendly vehicle.

When we walked outside, I noticed a smaller child asleep in a car seat inside her van.

"I think these would fit your price range,"

I said.

"These are nice," she said. After checking out a couple of the cars, the child then tugged on the woman's pant leg.

"Mommy, I want to play," the little girl said.

"That's fine," the woman said. "Just go check on your little sister first."

The woman and I continued to talk for a few more minutes, then we heard a little girl screaming. We turned toward the noise and noticed the older child running toward us in a panic like she'd just seen a ghost. She wasn't hurt, but she was definitely scared.

Then I noticed why she was screaming. Holy shit! The van was rolling backwards toward us and toward the busy highway. The woman let out a bloodcurdling scream.

Then realization set in. The younger child was still inside the vehicle. The van picked up speed, but the woman stood frozen. I rushed toward her, then pushed her out of the van's path.

"Get the fuck out of the way!" There was no way to stop a runaway van.

All of a sudden, the van jerked, then jerked again. It was like someone turned the steering wheel. The older child, who was running toward us, weaved between two vehicles when the van crashed into one of our cars. The van crushed the cars together, mere seconds after she passed through.

The woman ran to her van screaming. I noticed she was gripping her keys and the van's engine wasn't running. I wasn't sure how her vehicle came out of park in the first place. Most vehicles have a brake light switch connected to the brake. In order to get a vehicle out of park, the brake has to be pressed before the gearshift can be moved. That was how it worked. The switch was there to prevent vehicles from accidentally coming out of gear.

I called the police to report the accident and dispatch could hear the woman screaming in the background. She was so hysterical even her kids were shaking and crying. If the van had reached the highway and rolled into oncoming traffic, her younger child could've died. Her eldest child also could've been crushed between two vehicles. We could've been hit, too. The stress of all that was not going well, so I had to do something.

I approached the woman and her children and took control of the situation. I needed to get the kids away from their mom because her crying was making them more upset and they were already scared enough. By this time, the sleeping child was awake and was crying, too. I guided the kids into the office, changed the television channel to a cartoon program and gave them each a sucker. I explained to them that Mommy was just a little upset and needed some alone time.

Through her tear-streaked face, the elder child told me what happened. While her younger sibling was getting out of the van, she accidentally leaned on the gearshift and the car came out of park. I wasn't sure why the kids didn't use the side door instead of the driver's door, but they were just children. Besides, the van was turned off, it was in park and the woman had the keys.

When the police arrived, it was like the entire police force turned up. Sirens sounded and lights flashed. It was quite a commotion. The scene on the lot made passing motorists slow down on the highway.

After the police finished gathering information, one of the officers approached me. He asked me if I could allow the woman to leave her van parked on our lot. The van would be towed and impounded if not. Apparently, the woman had insurance, but her tags had recently expired and she hadn't had a chance to get to the county clerk's office, which she intended on doing that day. This only added to her anxiety. I felt bad for her.

The woman called her husband and he came

to pick her and the children up. It bothered her to relive the story, just as much as it bothered me to hear it. She was apologizing to me over and over because two of our vehicles were wrecked. I told her that's what insurance was for and not to worry about it. Everything would be fine.

I tried to lighten the mood. "If you're still interested in buying a car," I said. "I'll sell you one of those." I laughed a little and pointed toward the crushed vehicles, but she was too shaken up to see the humor in it.

My cell phone rang; it was Romeo calling during his lunch hour. I couldn't take his call because the police were still asking questions for their reports. I had to let it go to voicemail.

When I didn't answer my phone, Romeo would normally open the video surveillance app on his cell phone to see if I was super busy. If I was with customers, he would send me a 'thinking of you' text message.

When I didn't answer a second call, Romeo sent a text wanting to know what the hell was going on. He must have seen the police officers on the video and freaked out.

About ten minutes later, I managed to step away to call Romeo. As I listened to the ringing, I turned to scan the lot. The ringing stopped and Romeo's voicemail picked up.

It was at that moment, I saw Romeo's huge truck parked in the center turning lane. Shit. He was probably mad because I didn't take his call and came to see what the commotion was all about.

Romeo walked past the van that was still pushed against the two vehicles and his eyes locked onto mine. An officer tried to get his attention about his truck being parked in the center lane, but Romeo ignored him and continued to walk toward me.

By the look on his face, Romeo wasn't angry; he was concerned for me. Words were stuck in my throat and I couldn't talk. When Romeo was within arm's length, he didn't say anything. He just pulled me into a bear hug, wrapped his arms around me, then rested his chin on top of my head. Trying to keep my tears at bay, a sob escaped my mouth.

"I'm sorry," I whispered. "I couldn't take your call."

Romeo kissed the top of my head and hugged me tighter. "It's okay. You're okay."

The next day the woman and her husband arrived to pick up her van. I showed them the video I recorded on my cell phone, from the surveillance system recording. Romeo had reviewed the video after coming home during his lunch hour, yesterday. The man's eyes welled up as he watched seeing the danger everyone was in. He looked at me in horror. I thought he was going to faint.

"I didn't realize," he said, barely above a whisper.

"I told you," the woman said.

"But seeing it is different."

The couple asked me to forward the video to their cell phones and I did. After watching the video again, I knew angels were watching over those children, as well as the woman and me. From where the car started, it should have rolled right into the busy highway. Instead the van turned nearly 90 degrees to crash into two parked vehicles. The steering wheel should have stayed locked up because the keys weren't in the ignition, they were in the mother's hand. I couldn't explain it, but I was thankful nobody was hurt or killed. If someone actually died on our lot, I'd have gone absolutely bonkers.

I posted a sign on the office door that read: *Do not leave children unattended in vehicles. Ever.*

Chapter Eleven

♡

THINGS THAT GO BUMP

Up bright and early that Saturday morning, Romeo and I had a list of chores we both wanted to get done. I managed to start a load of laundry and watched the lot, while Romeo mowed the lawn and did other outside chores.

After starting a second load of laundry, I walked to the mailbox to retrieve the mail. On my way back, I saw Romeo carrying an A-Frame ladder to the front of the house.

"What are you doing?" I asked

"I'm going to clean out the gutters," he said, then opened the ladder and climbed up. Apparently, Romeo didn't have the ladder exactly where he wanted it, so he gripped the sides and lifted the ladder as he jumped. In doing so he moved the ladder over a few inches with each hop.

"That can't be safe," I said.

"I know what I'm doing," Romeo grunted, then climbed up to the top step.

"I don't think you're supposed to use the top step. It's not safe. You could fall."

"I've been using ladders for years. I know what I'm doing," he replied, then reached inside the gutter and began scooping out clumps of leaves.

Just then a vehicle pulled onto the lot and I made my way toward the office. The customer wanted to test-drive a vehicle to buy for his daughter. I retrieved the key and made a copy of his driver's license, while he filled out the test-drive form.

After the customer drove away, I went back to the house and began loading the dishwasher. Suddenly I heard a long scraping sound and then a loud thump. I stepped closer to the video surveillance monitor, but didn't see anything out of the ordinary. But then a small truck pulled onto the lot and parked out front. A man got out and ran toward the front of our house—not the office door. That was odd.

I dried my hands, then rushed outside to see

what was going on. Perhaps he knew Romeo, saw him on the ladder and wanted to stop for a visit. But the man didn't walk toward our home, he ran. I picked up my pace, then rounded the corner and saw Romeo sitting on the pavement with his head in his hands. His phone was on the ground next to the fallen ladder.

"What happened?" I asked, scanning Romeo for any obvious injuries.

Romeo only shook his head.

"I was driving by," the man said. "And saw him lose his balance and fall. He hit the ground hard."

"I'm fine," Romeo grumbled. He stood up, stretched his back and adjusted his shirt and shorts.

"Ladder-hopping again, huh?" I said, but Romeo didn't reply. "Maybe you should stay off the ladder for the rest of the day."

Just then, the customer who'd been on a test-drive pulled back onto the lot and I followed the vehicle to the parking space outside the office door.

"There's a strange smell coming from the car," he said. He handed me the key. "And it doesn't have much power to it."

"A smell coming from where?" I asked.

"I don't know. I'm not a mechanic."

I walked around the car and noticed some smoke coming from the back wheels—it smelled like something burning. I opened the driver side door, knelt down and noticed the emergency brake was engaged and pushed to the floor.

"Did you drive with the emergency brake on?" I asked.

"I don't know. I didn't touch it," he said.

"Well, you drove with it on," I said, holding back a laugh. "That's why it felt like the car didn't have much power. The smell is coming from the rear brakes."

Brake Man's face turned a shade of red and he declined my offer to let him drive it again.

Romeo ignored our conversation as he walked by, with a hacksaw in his hand. Oh, shit.

"What's he up to now?" I mumbled and watched him go toward one of the trees in the front yard.

The customer and I went inside the office. I handed him a business card, along with some additional information, should he be interested in coming back to buy the vehicle.

A few minutes later, I heard a clang and a loud shriek. I stood and peeked out the office window and saw Romeo bent over, holding his legs. I hurried outside to find Romeo groaning in pain and cursing under his breath. The hacksaw was on the ground next to some cut tree limbs.

"What happened, now?" I asked. Then I noticed hundreds of deep scratches on his inner thighs. Some were beginning to bleed.

"I was standing on a branch and it broke," he said.

"Maybe you shouldn't have been standing on it, in the first place." I followed him inside to help clean his wounds.

After Romeo's legs were cleaned and slathered with ointment, I used my cell phone to take a photo of his injuries.

"Why take a picture?" Romeo asked.

"I need proof," I said.

"Proof for what?"

"Proof that you were sliding down a tree in your shorts. Otherwise, nobody would believe me. I'm going to start documenting the stupid things that you do." I giggled.

"You better not."

"Then maybe you should stay on the ground for the rest of the day," I teased. "What other plans do you have?"

"Why?"

"It's apparent I can't leave you alone today."

Romeo rolled his eyes and walked outside.

As I was sweeping the kitchen floor, I saw

Romeo walk by the back door carrying a bucket. "What in the world is he up to now?" I asked Foxy Boxy. She only wagged her tail in reply. "I should probably lock up the power tools," I mumbled.

Curious, I glanced outside and saw Romeo scooping water out of the swimming pool. The rain from the previous day had filled the pool to the top.

It was such a hot summer that Romeo purchased a pool from Wal-Mart to help cool us down. It was easy to setup, too. As water filled the pool, the wide air filled ring on top lifted upward.

"At least he's on the ground," I said to Foxy Boxy, then tossed her a treat and went back to sweeping the floor.

As I was putting the broom away, I heard a swoosh-swoosh-swooooooosh sound. I didn't think anything of it until Romeo walked through the back door. He was completely drenched from head-to-toe and dripping water onto the entry mat. I couldn't help it, I laughed so hard I had to wipe the tears from my eyes.

"Wait! Before you tell me what happened," I said, then whipped out my phone and took a photo. "Proof!" I laughed some more.

Romeo didn't laugh. He reached into his

pockets and pulled out his dripping phone and soggy wallet.

"Maybe it still works?" I giggled, then tossed him a kitchen hand towel. "So, tell me. What happened?"

Romeo wiped his face and arms.

"I was using a bucket to scoop out the water, but it was easier to push down on the top of the pool. It was going great until I pushed down too far. The side wall went down and the weight of the water pushed me across the yard."

I peeked outside and saw the pool flat on the ground. "At least you got the water out." I couldn't help but giggle. Romeo was not amused.

"So," I said. "What else do you have planned today?"

"Not a damn thing," Romeo said, then sloshed through the house.

Chapter Twelve

A WALKIN MAN'S FRIEND

The sun beamed down scorching rays one humid August day. Our air conditioner was working overtime. I stepped outside and sweat glistened on my forehead and trickled down my face. The droplets created a deluge that burned and blinded me with salt and decorated my eyes with a lovely, mascara-smeared raccoon look.

People say, that it's not the heat, it's the humidity that will kill you. Whichever one was my killer, I didn't care for it one bit. If I had to be this hot, then I needed to be in a swimming pool or on a beach somewhere with the sounds of the ocean and a breeze to cool me down.

After Romeo had accidentally emptied our pool of water, he decided to pack it away until next year. So a quick dip in the pool during my lunch hour was out of the question.

Just like snow days, workers should be allowed to take hot days too. If it got much hotter, then I was going to go to the neighbor's house and accidentally fall into their swimming pool. Of course, I'd accidentally drop my phone just before falling in. I wasn't sure how I'd explain being in their backyard. That part might get a little messy. I blamed the heat and the humidity for my thoughts of trespassing. They were both equally responsible.

If I went outside for any amount of time and came back inside, it felt great, but within minutes I was hot again. I did everything I could to battle the heat like plugging in extra fans, placing a dripping cold washcloth on the back of my neck and sipping on a large glass of ice water. Nothing really cooled me down.

Usually on extremely hot days or blasted cold days, we weren't that busy, but occasionally a customer would come to test-drive and buy a vehicle.

At the hottest point of the day, I heard the creak of the office door and a gentleman entered. It caught me off guard because I normally knew when someone drove onto our lot. The video cameras and the faint bell sound from the driveway alert system kept me informed about visitors. I glanced at the video monitor looking for his vehicle, but I didn't see one in the parking customer lot.

The customer's face was flushed and his shirt was drenched in sweat. He reached into the front pocket of his shorts and pulled out a red shop rag, then wiped away the sweat on his face and the back of his neck. This guy wasn't retirement age yet, but my guess said he was very close.

"Hi, I'm Julia," I greeted him. "How are you, today?"

"Hot," the man said as he exhaled. "It sure does feel good in here."

"Did you walk?" I asked.

"Yes. That's why I'm here. I need a car."

I invited the customer to have a seat across from my desk to talk about a few vehicles. He looked like he was going to pass out from heat exhaustion. I pointed a fan in his direction, offered him a cold bottle of water, and purposely took my time answering his questions. The guy needed to cool down. I wasn't sure how far he walked to get to our lot. In his current condition, if he didn't buy a vehicle, I was going to drive him back home or at least pay for a taxi. There was no point making him endure the heat like he did when he walked here.

About fifteen minutes and two bottles of water later, the gentleman felt better and was ready to test-drive a vehicle. I walked him to the car he was most interested in, handed him the keys and told him to drive safe. I was glad he chose to test-drive a vehicle with good air conditioning.

I made my way back to the office and gulped down another bottle of water and directed the fan back in my direction. Glancing out the window, I noticed the customer hadn't left yet. He appeared to be playing with the radio and figuring out all the buttons and options. He was probably enjoying the cool air blowing on his face too.

I was bombarded with phone calls—sales calls and customer calls—which took up a good fifteen minutes of my time. After that I made a visit to Sir Johnny, because I had already gulped down a gallon of water since my last visit to the bathroom. When I returned to my desk, I glanced at the video monitor out of habit and noticed the customer was still in the vehicle. The driver's door was open and his left foot was planted on the ground. I wasn't sure if he still hadn't left yet or if he was just returning. I walked over to the window for a better look and waited a few more moments for any sign of movement. Nothing.

I placed my phone in my back pocket and made my way to the car. I didn't like pushy sales people, but if the customer needed my help to figure something out or had questions about a certain option, I was there to help. I've had people get in a vehicle, then get out because it wasn't comfortable enough or they couldn't figure out how to start it. Nothing surprised me anymore.

As I approached the running car, I noticed the man's hair blowing from the fan. The customer was leaning to one side and it looked like he was trying to get a better look at something on the center dash controls. As I got closer, I noticed his eyes were closed, like he was taking a nap, but his skin tone was now a gray-bluish color.

I jerked the driver's door all the way open, which hit the car next to it with a loud thud. I started shaking the man's left arm and asked if he was okay, but he didn't respond. Shaking him only caused his body to slump even more toward the center console.

"Sir, can you hear me?" I asked, but he didn't move. Shit.

I whipped out my cell phone, called 911 and explained the situation. The calm dispatch officer said an ambulance was already on its way to my location.

"Just stay calm," she said. "Is he breathing?"

By the color of the customer's skin, he wasn't getting the proper amount of oxygen if any, but she wanted me to make sure. I turned off the blower fan, placed my finger under his nose but didn't feel anything, then I leaned in close and listened for breathing.

"Um, I'm not sure."

I've watched enough television shows to know that putting a mirror under a person's nose could pick up the slightest sign of breathing by fogging the mirror. The problem was I didn't have a mirror. But I did have a snazzy smartphone. I made the screen go black, then held the phone under his nose. Still, nothing. The man wasn't breathing. A cry of panic escaped my mouth and I was on the verge of an asthma attack.

"He's not breathing!" I yelled, then stepped back.

"You need to remain calm," the dispatcher said in a firm tone.

"I'm calm!" I yelled again.

My hands were shaking and I was freaking out. But I knew I had to do everything I could to help this man. Tears threatened to fall, but I swiped at my eyes and held it together. I could cry later.

"Can you lay him flat?" the dispatcher asked.

I contemplated that question for a moment. I could probably get him out of the vehicle, but I might hurt him doing it. Plus, the customer was much bigger than me and the car was parked between two other vehicles. "There's no way I can get him out of the car."

"Can you lay the seat all the way back?"

I hadn't thought of that. The emergency lady was a genius. I placed one hand on the side of the seat near the headrest and pulled the release handle, then eased him back. I rushed to the other side of the car, flung the door open, which hit the other car, and climbed inside. The door handle had come off in my hand and I threw it on the floorboard. "Cheap plastic parts," I mumbled. I made a mental note to deal with that shit later.

"Do you know how to perform CPR?" she asked. I didn't want to let her down.

"I've watched it on television," I replied. "Does that count?"

"It's okay," she said. "I can talk you through the steps."

At that moment, I heard emergency sirens approaching. A police car arrived first and whipped onto the car lot. I could see the confusion on his face as he scanned the property, not sure where to go.

Thankfully dispatch was still on the phone and I told her to direct the officer toward the far end of the car lot. I climbed out of the car and started waving my arms in the air and yelling to get his attention. The officer noticed me and drove over in his cruiser. He leaped out of his car and rushed to the passenger side of the vehicle and began his own evaluation. Within seconds he tilted the customer's head back, pulled a plastic mask out from somewhere, placed it over the customer's mouth, and then started CPR. It all happened so fast.

An ambulance pulled onto the lot next and two EMTs rushed over with their life-saving equipment.

Another police officer arrived on the scene but parked his vehicle in the center lane of the highway with the emergency lights flashing. He met up with the first officer, then made his way toward me. He held a clipboard and wanted more details, so I started from when the customer first arrived.

Within minutes the customer was placed on a gurney and the EMTs rolled the stretcher toward the ambulance. One of the EMTs squeezed a breathing bulb to supply oxygen while they moved him.

"Is he going to be okay?" I asked the officer.

"He's in good hands," I heard the officer say.

"Can you let me know?"

"Sure, no problem."

I handed the officer a business card. Vehicles on the highway slowed nearly to a stop as they passed our lot. I couldn't blame them. I had a feeling this would end up all over social media within minutes, if it hadn't already.

I watched as the ambulance eased onto the highway then sped away with its sirens blaring and both police cruisers following close behind.

I made my way back to the car where the incident occurred to put the seat back into the correct position and retrieve the keys. The customer's sweaty shop rag was wedged between the front seats, and the broken door handle was still on the floorboard where I had tossed it.

I went back to the office to cool down and sort through what had happened. If I had paid better attention to the customer while he was outside, I could have helped him sooner. I needed to hear a calm voice, so I called Ginger and filled her in on the details.

"You did the right thing, Jules," she said. "That's just lousy luck."

She was right, but it was hard not to feel a little responsible.

"He just seemed so nice," I said.

"Maybe you'll hear from him soon—might even buy the car."

I laughed. Ginger could always put my mind at ease.

About 30-minutes into our conversion, my phone beeped in with another call and I ended our conversation. It was the officer who questioned me after the incident.

"He didn't make it, Julia," the officer informed me. "I'm sorry."

I don't mind texting Romeo at work with funny stuff, but I hated bothering him with serious shit. Most things could wait until he called me during his lunch break or after he got home. It would be just my luck that Romeo would find out about emergency vehicles at the lot, and he'd assume I was hurt. I decided to send him a text message.

Me: Someone died on the lot today.
Romeo: OMG! Who did you kill?

I didn't have time to reply before the phone rang. Romeo wanted to know who I murdered and why. He was probably worried I was about to go to jail and he needed to bail me out or hire a criminal attorney. I calmed him down and explained what had happened.

Romeo was silent, probably trying to wrap his mind around what I had told him. So I took the opportunity to continue the one-sided conversation and started bombarding him with my thoughts.

"Do we need to lower the price of that vehicle because someone died in it?" I lamented how the old man's ghost would probably haunt the car and was concerned his death would end up on the vehicle report. Full disclosure. Or maybe it could be a new ad campaign: "Deals so good you'll have a heart attack."

I'd never been witness to someone dying before my eyes. Well, not a freshly dead person, anyway. Funeral homes didn't count because I would go inside knowing a person had passed away. It was totally different.

After I hung up the phone, I heard a noise, which sounded like the office door opening.

"Hello?" I said, then scanned the video surveillance monitor, but nobody was there. It might have been the wind, but I suspected unfinished ghost business.

I wasn't taking any chances. I closed the office for the rest of the day and went home. I needed some wine. I blamed the ghost.

Chapter Thirteen

SOMETIMES I NEED A BREAK

When I felt the lingering stress of the house-work not getting done again, I took more notice of my stress levels and tried to head them off by taking Thursday to just do the little things that weighed heavy on my mind. Sometimes, doing projects or cleaning was a great way to take my mind off the car lot and helped lessen my worries.

It was a rare occasion when I told Romeo that I was going to take a Thursday off instead of going to the dealer auction. Officially the office was closed anyway. I only did it when I knew it was time for a break. It was my body's way of telling me to calm the fuck down or be admitted to an asylum. It was cheaper to take a day off. At least that's what the health insurance company would say and I'd have to agree with them.

So I announced to Romeo I wanted to take a day off. I planned to get a pedicure and have my nails polished, then come back home and clean the house. It had been months since I had my nails done. I wanted to feel cute and having my gray roots colored the previous month only went so far. I was beginning to look my age and I wasn't ready.

Romeo just laughed.

"I'm serious," I said.

"Of course you are." He didn't look up from his show, probably thinking that I was still joking.

"It's been a while, and I need some me-time."

"Yeah, you've been working hard," he said. He still didn't sound convinced, but I was taking the day off and I meant it.

I went to bed at midnight, and I was happy knowing that I didn't have to go to the dealer sale in the morning. I was totally excited to have a day to myself.

I woke up early, without an alarm, which was quite shocking. I hated getting up early and I was usually late for sale day. But that day

I was excited to get ready for my day off, like a kid on Christmas morning. I leaped out of bed with eye-opening energy, took Foxy Boxy out for her morning relief and proceeded to get ready. Happiness ran through my veins. I was hooked up to an IV of ecstasy.

First, I wanted to drink an entire cup of coffee. That was a luxury because I never had time to drink the whole thing before it got cold. My coffee was like liquid gold. As I entered the kitchen, I zoned in on the electric kettle and ignored everything around me. By the time I was dressed, the water would be at the perfect temperature for my coffee and I could start my day off the right way.

Wrong.

I filled the kettle with fresh water and set a mug on the counter in front of it, then turned to go get ready. As I was passing the lateral file cabinet with the printer on top, I noticed a paper in the printer tray. I reached for it, but already knew what it was. My heart sank. My wonderful husband printed a list of certain vehicles available for sale in today's auction. I wasn't going to get my day off. Romeo thought I was joking after all.

I loved my husband with my entire being. Romeo meant the world to me and I don't know what I'd do without him. But sometimes he didn't know when I was at my breaking point. I didn't usually want to share that bit of information with him because it made me appear weak. In general, I wasn't a weak person. I ran a car lot and I dealt with a bunch of shit every single day. I'm strong and independent and successful. I'm awesome that way!

It's just that sometimes I really needed a day off. Everyone does, except Romeo. He's like Superman, Spiderman and the Energizer Bunny all wrapped up in one. Yeah, he's a Super Husband and he doesn't even break a sweat. He claimed it's because he uses a ton of salt and drinks his iced tea extra sweet. He might be onto something, but I'd never admit to it.

I put my glasses on and sent Romeo a text message. I wanted to know about the list he printed and if he truly wanted me to attend the auction. He replied almost immediately that he wanted me to at least attend the online auction. Last week, I bought vehicles online because it was way too hot and humid to actually attend the auction. Humidity made it harder for me to breathe—like I was drowning in thick air. It was just one small perk of having asthma and refusing to use the prescribed inhaler and medication. I did not sign up as a guinea pig for pharmaceutical companies to have doctors try various medications on me. I was a badass ninja warrior and my lungs better start believing it.

I shook my head while I looked at the list. The last vehicle listed was run number 125. On average it took at least a minute and a half for each vehicle to run through the sale. It didn't sound like a lot, but when auctioneers had over 1,000 vehicles to sell, it added up. I knew it would be at least noon before I was finished with the online auction. I was thankful the last vehicle Romeo wanted me to watch wasn't number 500. I took a deep breath and went to the bathroom to finish getting ready for my not-getting-my-day-off day.

I turned on the bathroom faucet and started to cry, but not just a little teary-eyed cry. No, I mean, I really sobbed—with bloodshot eyes and huge tears. I tried shaking it off, and started crying all over again. I cried four times by the time I finished getting ready. I wasn't sure what the hell was going on with me. I felt sorry for myself and at the same time like a spoiled child not getting what she wanted and throwing a tantrum. I was just shy of falling on the floor kicking and screaming. I didn't need a pedicure that bad, for Christ's sake. I felt stupid. I started crying again when I remembered the nail salon I went to didn't take appointments. They were walk-ins only.

When I made it back to the kitchen, I poured a cup of coffee and then got my laptop set up on the kitchen table. I sat down with the list and I started crying again. The only thing running through my mind at the start of that crying fit was how selfish I had been in wanting a day off.

Romeo got up for work each morning and never missed a day unless it was a planned vacation. He never complained. He never needed to have a day to himself. So, yeah, I felt ashamed of being a selfish person.

After chastising myself and pulling myself together, I started crying again because I started thinking about the guy who tried to steal his car back, the runaway van with the kid inside, and the man who died on our lot. My mind was all over the place. It took me seven years to convince Romeo to close on Sunday and I was tired after dealing with people all day long, six days a week. I really needed that Thursday off.

It was noon before I was done with the online auction. I ended up purchasing three vehicles. Whatever. My day was already ruined, in my opinion. I wanted to get my personal care done in the morning, then clean the house in the afternoon. There was no way

I'd get everything done now.

I went to the nail salon and sat outside for fifteen minutes coughing up a lung. That's asthma for you. I began to wonder if I was being selfish because I was spending Romeo's hard earned money to get my nails done. So, I started to get all teary-eyed, again. I sat in my car a little longer than planned to pull myself together, then went inside. I ended up with the older woman who takes forever. Like two hours forever. My day wasn't going as planned anyway.

After my nails were finished, I found myself sitting in my vehicle and trying to decide my next move. I could go to the grocery store and buy something to cook for dinner, or I could just say screw it and buy fast food tonight. Honestly, the dinner I wanted to cook would be much more enjoyable if I were drinking wine while I cooked it. But after this morning, I decided wine wouldn't be a good idea. I wasn't happy, yet. Getting my nails done made me feel spoiled. The guilt weighed heavily on my mind. Fast food it was.

Romeo called on his way home and I told him what happened that morning. "You said 'yeah, you've been working hard' but then there was the list," I said between gasps for breath. I could barely explain myself without crying.

"I'm not sure what you want me to say," he said. "How can we talk about this when you're so emotional?"

That only made me cry again, but I kept my voice steady so he didn't know. I didn't even mention that I purchased three vehicles. Something wasn't right with me that day. I was broken, or at least a little fractured.

Tears flowed down my cheeks, but I told Romeo I was fine. I hung up the phone and wiped my tears away. I was screaming inside my head. I wanted to talk to someone who would understand what I was going through, but I knew I would just say that I was fine. I was always fine.

On my way home, I wondered why I continued to run the car lot or even if it was worth it anymore. But through all the bull-shitters, jerks and people who have screwed us over, there were some genuinely nice people out there. Those good, hard working people made our car lot worth every breakdown I had.

Romeo arrived home while I was in the office dealing with the vehicles I purchased. He went straight to the garage, worked on cars and got them ready for the lot. He worked hard all day and came home to do more work on the lot. He was tired, too. I knew it. He needed a day off just as bad as I did, but he would never admit it. That was probably why he didn't understand my morning breakdown.

Over the past several years, I've found that if I read books during our busiest season—when people received their tax refunds—it helped me keep my sanity and I stayed much calmer. The books I'd been reading were full of kick-ass chicks. Time and again, for brief transits in my mind or for longer periods wafting through my soul, I found myself continuing to self-identify with that classic female warrior type, so often the protagonist in the stories I love to read.

My true medieval ninja warrior princess inner being was clawing and begging to break out of my car dealership dungeon. I felt like that part of me could take anyone down. I desperately wanted to covertly slide the key under the massive door to her dungeon cell and let her out to play my medieval version of Lara Croft. She would wield a sword made from a ball-peen hammer and kick some serious ass.

If my morning was any indication of how I'd do in battle, I'd flunk out, big time. Maybe, I should Google swordsmanship or archery classes in my area. It wouldn't hurt to be prepared for an alien invasion, just in case. After my minor meltdown that morning, piano lessons were probably more appropriate. If I worked on the lot six days all the time and melted down every seventh, I wouldn't have time for saving the world anyway.

I was in the kitchen replying to emails, when Romeo walked inside. If he wanted to start examining what I went through that morning, I was liable to start crying again. We didn't talk much, which was strange. To be truthful, he probably didn't know what to say and neither did I.

I was suddenly curious if we were having a full moon. It wouldn't surprise me to find out that lunar activity was to blame for my unusual behavior. It wouldn't surprise me to find out that the moon influenced crazy people. I made a mental note to Google that after I finished up with the emails.

I hoped that whatever happened that morning would just go away and never come back. Romeo sat in the living room and soon after, I heard snoring. Yeah, he was tired, which made me feel even shittier.

I visited Sir Johnny and realized I started my period. Shit. I Googled my concerns about being so emotional at my age at the start of a period, and came up with "premenopausal." I didn't need a doctor, because I already figured it out. I saved the co-pay. I could put the money I saved toward investing in more projects to keep my sanity.

My self-diagnosed Googlecare totally worked. I could try contacting our government again and suggest they rename our national healthcare system to "Americare". It sounded more American and I loved it. Not that I would get paid for my super awesome idea.

I couldn't blame this morning's meltdown entirely on my hormones. Although, my hormones probably played a huge part.

Part of being a strong woman was being able to admit that I was weak and vulnerable at times. But it took super ninja strength to admit when I needed to stop for a rest. I finally realized that I was allowed to take a break. And I deserved it.

A nap sounded like a good idea. It would make this awful day go away. Besides, I needed to snap out of this weird funk. Off to bed I went. And sadly, no one got laid that night.

Chapter Fourteen

♡

DON'T PISS IN MY YARD

The phone started ringing the moment the office opened. An older gentleman with a rough voice responded to my greeting.

"I'm calling about a vehicle you have. I noticed the tire was plum flat. What are you going to do about it?"

I choked my laughter down. It sounded to me like he was calling about a flat tire instead of a car. I fielded his question like a professional.

"Air it up," I said.

A few hours later he showed up at the lot and wanted more information.

I still wore my air cast so I tried not to walk

too much because it caused more pain. The car he was interested in was parked at the far end of the lot. I forced myself to ignore the pain, picked up the air tank, then grabbed the jump box too—just in case the battery was dead. Sometimes a vehicle needs a jump if it hasn't been started in a while. It began to rain, so I took my time walking to the vehicle. A few close calls made me realize that my walking boot wasn't slip resistant.

The man didn't offer to carry anything. Instead he asked, "What do you need the jump box for?"

As much as I wanted to be a smart-ass, I had to concentrate on the slick pavement or I'd fall and break something.

"Just in case the battery is dead," I said.

The man tucked his hands into his pockets, still not offering to help carry anything. "In my experience, if you need to jump a car, then the battery needs to be replaced."

I slowed my pace and glanced up. I could hear he was looking for free upgrades: first the flat tire, and now a battery.

"That's not necessarily true," I said. "Sometimes the battery just needs to be charged."

We arrived at the vehicle and I set the jump box and air tank on the ground, then looked at the front tire. The tire he said was "plum flat" was only a little low. "Same stupid, different day," I mumbled. "Welcome to Stupidville."

Some people tended to exaggerate in hopes of getting free stuff. I was tired of people thinking they could get a new tire just because it was a little low, or a new paint job because of a scratch.

Instead of me hauling the air tank to the truck, it would've been easier to move the truck near the garage instead. I narrowed my eyes at the guy.

"I thought you said the tire was 'plum flat.'" I lugged the air tank out, because I believed the man when he said the tire was flat. What a waste of my time.

He shifted and took a few steps back. "I didn't mean it was flat, flat," he said, trying his best to look innocent.

"What did you mean?" I pressed, holding his gaze.

"That it needed a little air," he said, then looked away.

Peter Pan came to mind and I wondered if I could send him an email and ask if he had this guy's marbles. I knelt down and used the air tank to put five pounds of air into the low tire while the customer watched. Five pounds wouldn't even make the tire pressure sensor light come on. I could've aired it up with the

HILTON

steam coming out of my ears.

I handed the key to Flat Guy and asked him to start the vehicle. It started right up without the aid of the jump box. Flat Guy scrunched his nose. He was surely hoping to get a new battery. Not this time.

I watched Flat Guy play with the different options on the center console. He turned every knob and pushed and jabbed extra hard on every button, just to see what they did. If Flat Guy continued to push the knobs that hard, he was liable to break one.

Then it happened. The bastard broke one off and held it up for me to see. There was something seriously wrong with that man. I'd bet my chocolate he'd want me to pay for it and he was the one who broke it. "Did you see that?"

"Yes, I did," I said, and gripped the door-frame.

"Are you going to fix it?"

"Yes. And I'm going to add the repair cost to the price of the vehicle."

I supposed he didn't like my reply, because he handed me the key and the broken knob.

"I'll think about it."

After Flat Guy left, three cars and a van pulled onto the lot and parked. They were the vehicles I had purchased on sale day from the online auction. It was rare, but sometimes the cars were driven in instead of hauled. As I was signing for the delivery, I noticed one of the three drivers, an older man, was missing. I scanned the lot, then noticed him hovering just behind the garage where Romeo parked his personal car.

We had boundaries. Streamers, signs and parking lines indicated where the car lot was located. People sometimes snooped around at the fringes, violating our privacy.

I started walking toward him. "Hey! That car isn't for sale."

The guy turned his head toward me and just grinned a little. He didn't move his arms, like the rest of his body was involved in something he couldn't break away from. Suddenly, I knew what he was doing and stopped in my tracks. I didn't want to actually see what he was doing.

That old fart was taking a piss on our property. It wasn't like he was on a hiking trip in the woods, where nobody would accidentally see him. Besides we had a bathroom and there was a McDonald's just down the road.

"What the hell are you doing?" I asked, but I already knew. "We have a bathroom you know."

"Sorry, but I had to go real bad." He turned around and adjusted his zipped up pants.

"That's no excuse!" My yelling got the attention of the other drivers. "You can't just go around pissing wherever you feel like it."

Apparently, it was raining stupid people today. It could be some type of stupid-virus or an epidemic the Centers for Disease Control didn't know about, but stupid was growing faster than weeds. If a stupid-virus vaccine wasn't offered to the public soon, we would all be vulnerable. I had a fleeting thought that I should send the CDC an email and maybe the pharmaceutical companies, too. Instead, as soon as the delivery drivers left, I called the dealer auction and told the transportation supervisor what Piss-N-Boots did on our property. Needless to say, the supervisor was shocked. I told him I didn't want that idiot to step foot on our car lot, again.

Could my day get any worse?

Not even a minute later, another vehicle pulled onto the lot. I slumped my shoulders, because I had to visit Sir Johnny and I wasn't sure how much longer my bladder could hold out. Just thinking about it made me cross my legs. I wasn't wiggling or hopping up and down yet, so that was a good sign.

It might have been a good idea to invest in some super absorbent adult diapers. A Google search stated they were quite the fashion nowadays and some of them looked quite sexy with lace. But alas, a diaper was a diaper no matter how sexy they looked, lace or not.

The state inspector stepped out of her car. What now? No warning. No email. No courtesy call to notify me of her pending arrival. This chick was pretty cool last time, but I was wary after the day I'd had so far.

It was strange how an unexpected visit from the state inspector made me want to go pee even more. I was seriously reevaluating my thoughts about those lace diapers.

After we made ourselves comfortable in the office, I began telling her about the past week, including today's stupidity. If anyone would believe me, it would be her. I'd bet someone else's money she's heard a ton of outrageous stories that happened to other car dealers.

After listening to what I had to say, she leaned in all serious and said, "Prozac helps with that."

I busted out laughing and tears filled my eyes. That was just the funny comment I needed to get through the rest of the day.

Although the Prozac comment was hilarious, I didn't like taking medication and I certainly didn't need some psychiatrist trying to say I was crazy. Romeo already thought I was nuttier than a fruitcake and that would just confirm it. Wine helped with my stress and I was good with that.

I was fortunate to be able to talk to a woman in the car business that knew about the bullshit I was dealing with on a daily basis. Maybe she could become a traveling therapist and counsel women car dealers all over the state. She might as well, because she was already going to visit them anyway.

I briefly wondered what the state inspector would say if she saw a man taking a piss outside a car lot. I giggled at the thought. She'd probably wait until the guy was finished doing his business, hand him a card, then fine the transportation company up the ass.

Chapter Fifteen

♡

FREE PARTS

By the time I finished my first cup of coffee, I noticed a vehicle parked near the office door. The office didn't open for another fifteen minutes and I wasn't in a big hurry to start my day. As I poured a second cup of coffee, I watched another vehicle pull onto the lot and park.

"Today is going to be a busy day," I murmured to Foxy Boxy, which somehow excited her and made her start jumping around like a rabbit. She probably thought I was offering her a treat. I looked at her cute puppy-dog eyes and caved. "I might as well go see what they want." I sighed, then tossed her a treat.

As I walked toward the office door, I noticed

an SUV pull onto the lot and park near the entrance. The first customer simply wanted to make a payment, only taking a few minutes of my time.

The second customer wanted more information about a truck parked near the garage, not ready for sale, yet. It was a repo vehicle.

"I'd like to know how much your husband would sell that truck for?" she asked.

Oh, my goddess, another woman who thought only a man could run a car lot. If she continued with the only-a-man-can-run-a-car-lot attitude, I'd have to teach her a lesson.

"I can give you a price," I said in a cheerful tone. "One thousand dollars, plus the transfer costs—which includes the sales tax—and it's all yours," I said.

By the look on her face, I knew the price was too good for her to pass up. Even with the higher miles, it was a four-wheel drive and the truck retailed for five times that amount. It was a repo and I didn't mind selling it cheaper. One person's loss was another's gain. The truck needed to be cleaned up, and have the exterior driver's door handle replaced, but the low price more than compensated for that. The handle could be purchased on eBay for about twenty dollars. I wasn't sure if it needed any mechanical work, but Tiny didn't indicate any problems when he brought it to the lot. Even if the truck needed some work, it was still worth it, as is.

As she made her way to the truck, I glanced at the SUV parked near the entrance and noticed a young man making his way toward me. The truck lady would be fine for a few minutes without me, so I decided to meet the young man halfway.

"I'd like to test-drive that SUV in the front row," he said. He gestured toward it as he approached me.

"Okay, I'll go get the key." I made my way back toward the office.

Truck Lady was hot on my heels and followed me inside. "Are you going to clean it?" she asked.

"No," I said. "For that price, you can clean it yourself." Truck Lady looked hurt. It wouldn't kill her to take it home and clean it herself or run it through a car wash. "If you want us to detail it, then I'm going to raise the price another hundred bucks. Your choice." That got her thinking. Almost positive she would want to take it for a ride, I snatched the truck key and slid it into my pocket just in case. I pointed to the guy waiting outside. "Let me give that customer this key, so he can go on a test-drive. I'll be right back."

As I made my way toward the young man, a woman got out of the passenger side of their SUV, walked around, and hopped into the driver's seat. I was concerned someone might whip their vehicle into the drive and asked him if she could move it to a parking spot.

"It's a little dangerous being parked at the entrance," I said. I handed him the key and he asked about our financing. I answered his questions and let him know that we had recently replaced the battery.

The woman began moving their vehicle and I assumed she would be waiting here until he returned. Their SUV was the same make and model of the one the young man wanted to test-drive, although it was a different color. I took another look and it didn't have a plate on the back, but it did have a sticker for another car lot here in town.

"Are you test-driving that vehicle?" I asked, as he started the SUV.

"Yeah," He replied.

"Let me get this straight," I lowered my voice. "You're test-driving two of the same SUVs from two different dealers at the same time?"

"Yes, we're taking them to my grandfather so he can look them over. He works at the mechanic shop down the road." He pointed down the road, toward the outskirts of town. "I'll be back in twenty minutes."

At that moment, the woman pulled the SUV onto the highway and sped away. "Where's she going? If no one is staying here, you need to fill out a test-drive form," I said. Then I saw the truck lady coming my way.

"How much longer are you going to be?" she yelled and waived. "I have some questions." She then placed an impatient hand on her hip.

"I'll be right with you." I looked at the young man. "Test-drives are only fifteen minutes, but I'll allow you twenty. Let me take a picture of your driver's license." I whipped out my cell phone. He didn't fill out the test-drive form, but a copy of his license was better than nothing. The only mechanic past our car lot was the new one that opened up a few weeks ago. SUV Guy looked like an average, clean-cut dude, so I wasn't that worried.

Truck Lady was pacing near the repo vehicle she'd inquired about as I approached her. "It needs a door handle," she said, pointing toward the broken handle.

"Yes, it does."

"Are you going to fix it?"

"No, not for the price I gave you." I leaned against the fender.

"I'll come back. When your husband is here," she sneered. "So he can open the door for me."

Stupid people drive me insane. I'm sure everyone runs into them, not the same ones I've had the luxury of meeting, but similar idiots. It's possible the frequent appearances of these characters might be related in some way. It could be an alien conspiracy to secretly force mankind to kill each other. The government could be creating armies of stupid people just to see what happens to the human race. And for some reason they gravitated to our car lot.

I ignored her brainless comment.

"I can open the door," I said, then walked around to the passenger side, got in and opened the driver's door from the inside. She slid into the driver's seat and I handed her the key. When she tried it, the engine wouldn't start. The battery was dead.

"I'll come back when your husband can jump-start the truck," she said, then got out.

"I can jump-start the truck," I replied. I went and retrieved the portable jump-box from the garage. I popped open the hood, hooked up the cables and asked her to start the truck. Viola! It started right up. "The battery probably just needs to be charged. It's been sitting a while. No big deal."

"It barely has any gas in it." She pointed at the dashboard. She turned off the truck, got out and shut the door. "I'll come back when your husband can put some gas in it." She flipped her hair over her shoulder.

"I can put gas in it," I said. Maybe she wanted to speak to Romeo in hopes of getting an even lower price, or to talk him into fixing the door handle and detailing it for free. It wouldn't surprise me if she wanted to flirt with Romeo to get her way.

Apparently, I was such a lame female that I didn't know how to give a price, open a door, start it or even put gas in it. In that moment, I began to lose faith in the human race, especially the stupid ones. They're kind of hard to pick out until they open their mouths to speak.

"I'll come back when your husband is here," she said.

It was time to put Truck Lady in her place. I looked her in the eye, then raised my voice. "*I'm* the one who runs this car lot. *Not* my husband. If you *really* need his assistance, he'll be here when he gets off work. He comes here to *help* me."

Her eyes grew wide and she took a step back. She knew she had crossed a line and pushed me too far. "Well, a friend of mine might be interested in this truck."

I took a deep breath to calm down. "Then your friend needs to be the one to come look at it." I smirked at her, then held out my hand for the key. If looks could kill, she would've had me hung from a tree and skinned alive. And I would've stamped the word "stupid" across her forehead.

When the truck lady left, the SUV Guy still hadn't returned, so I went back to the office and started doing some title work to prepare recently sold vehicles for transfer at the County Clerk's Office. If I didn't have the paperwork filled out and ready, we'd be charged an extra fee.

After finishing the paperwork, I glanced at my watch. I couldn't believe it had been nearly two hours since SUV Guy had left. Paperwork and phone calls had kept me distracted and busy. I grabbed the key to a mini-van and decided to take a drive toward the new mechanic shop down the road. Maybe Grandpa was slow at inspecting vehicles.

As I approached the new shop, I pulled across the street and parked in front of a vacant building. The new mechanic shop across the street had four bay doors, and they were all open. One was empty, while the other three bays had three different color SUVs parked in them.

One was ours. One was the SUV the woman was driving when she sped away from our lot. The other—slightly dirty—SUV was parked in between both of them. All three SUVs were different colors, but I'd bet Romeo's lunch money, they were the same make and model.

I pulled out my phone and started taking some photos, then began to record a video of the people moving around the vehicles. I saw SUV Guy and the woman standing nearby, while an older gentleman—who I could only assume was Grandpa—rolled a cart with tools and parts between the vehicles. Without being closer, I couldn't tell if the SUVs were the same year, but I'd put money down that the parts were interchangeable.

"You fucking bastards," I mumbled. "You are so busted." It took everything I had not to go all badass ninja on the part-stealing thieves. Instead, I reined in my emotions and dialed 911. Romeo would be so proud that I didn't approach them myself.

I informed the police of the shenanigans and I was instructed not to approach the assailants. I agreed and told dispatch that I had taken some photos and was currently recording the thieves in action, then I ended the call.

"You're so going down," I said through gritted teeth, then giggled in anticipation of their impending doom.

It felt like forever, but finally two police cruisers with lights and blaring sirens whipped into the mechanic's lot. The officers blocked the bay doors with their vehicles, then opened their driver doors and stood behind them, with their weapons drawn.

SUV Guy, the woman and Grandpa all raised their hands in the air. Moments later, three more police officers arrived on scene. From across the road, it appeared that there was some misunderstanding as the three would-be thieves talked to the officers. They weren't in handcuffs, yet and a whole lot of talking was going on.

Oh, my goddess. I hoped I didn't just call the police on innocent people. Just then, an officer crossed the road and approached me, while the rest of them looked on. Romeo wouldn't be happy if he had to bail me out of jail for mis-reporting a crime. Shit. Good thing I knew Ginger's number by heart. 1-800-GOT-FUNK. I'd call her instead.

The officer stated that SUV Guy was just test-driving vehicles while having his vehicle worked on. His grandfather was simply inspecting the vehicles. The officer guided me across the busy highway and my face flushed red with embarrassment as we approached the group of people staring at me. I indicated which SUV was ours and the officer walked me toward the front of it. SUV Guy was gone two hours. I knew something wasn't right.

"Please, tell me if you think anything is out of place," the officer said, then gestured toward our vehicle, the customer's vehicle and the tool cart.

As I stepped in front of the open hood, I noticed the alternator was gone. On the tool cart was a grimy old alternator and the one that had been in our vehicle was partially bolted to the SUV in the middle bay. The officer took note of my findings. Upon further inspection, there was an old battery installed in place of the new one we had purchased from the Auto Parts store just a few days earlier. Again, I looked under the hood of the SUV in the center bay and saw our new battery already hooked up. I looked at SUV Guy and grinned.

The police officer standing to my side, nodded his head and that was the go-ahead for the other officers to place handcuffs on SUV Guy, the woman and Grandpa.

The officer explained that he had a feeling something wasn't right, but I had to verify what they had found. If I hadn't caught them, they would have gotten away with it.

Just as the thieves were being placed in the

back of the cruisers, another vehicle pulled into the mechanic's lot. A guy stepped out of the vehicle, wearing work clothes and a name stitched on his shirt that read "Bubba." Bubba's hands and arms had traces of grease on them.

"What's going on?" he asked. He stared at Grandpa—probably his boss—in the back of the police car.

One of the police officers explained to Bubba what happened. Bubba then offered to switch the parts back.

I returned to our car lot to make a copy of the receipt for the recently purchased battery and took it back to the waiting officers. Our engine compartment was super-clean in comparison to the other SUV, so it wasn't hard to tell which parts were ours. I was glad to have proof of the battery purchase. It made a more solid case against the thieves.

Upon further questioning, Grandpa caved and admitted to switching the alternator, battery and the starter from our SUV. His grandson wanted him to take the radio from the other test-driven vehicle, but he hadn't gotten around to it.

Bubba finished replacing our parts and offered to drive the SUV back to our lot, but I had already called Ginger and she was waiting across the street. Bubba was still in shock about the entire situation. I forwarded the photos and video to the officer's phone and email. He then told me I would more than likely have to testify in court. I didn't mind.

After they left, Romeo called me on his lunch break.

"Hey, Babe. How's your day going?" He asked.

"Well, a woman wants to flirt with you to get a lower price on the repo truck," I said. "She also wants you to replace the handle and clean it, too."

"Is that all?"

"No. You'll be glad to know that I didn't go to jail, today," I said.

"Oh, my God. What did you do to her?"

"It wasn't her," I said. "I was a badass ninja. I stopped three thieves and I got it all on video. What do you have to say about that?"

"Start from the beginning," Romeo said.

"Well," I began, "I was drinking a cup of coffee and talking to Foxy Boxy. Everything was fine, until I opened the business."

Chapter Sixteen

CUSTOMER APPRECIATION

After my second cup of coffee the next morning, I had a brief meeting with Sir Johnny. Every time I got to the end of a roll of toilet paper I left about three squares. Those precious squares were not usable due to the adhesive refusing to allow them to detach from the tube. The business was open, the lights were on, and it was unusually slow. That meant I had some time to spare to research about my lost squares. I decided to go to my trusted Internet friend, Google, and look up toilet paper facts. I kept an eye on the video monitors and started my Google search.

What I found was a bit unsettling. A campaign was going around about tube-free toilet paper. After reading about that shit and doing the math, I was all for buying tube-free toilet paper.

Google revealed each person, on average, uses 57 squares of toilet paper per day. That adds up to an average of about 100 rolls per year. I'm assuming they were using single rolls with those statistics. With the amount of fluids I drank, I probably used more than that. By my calculations, I was losing about three rolls per year to those stuck-on squares. I figured the toilet paper companies owed me around 150 rolls due to unusable squares because I paid for the whole roll of toilet paper. When you added it all up, those three squares were important. It seemed like there could be potential for a class action lawsuit.

The cereal people wanted my breakfast to go stale and now the toilet paper people wanted my lady parts to drip dry. Google said I would spend an average of three years with Sir Johnny during my lifetime. I was curious as to how long the toilet paper people thought I was going to live.

I wondered if toilet paper statistics took loose bowel days into consideration. On those particular days, it seemed everyone was with Sir Johnny more often than usual.

I thought I should probably ask Romeo to install a television or an intercom system in the bathroom. If I was going to spend three years or more in there, I wanted to make the most of it. We probably needed to buy one of those cushioned seats, too. Sir Johnny would like that upgrade and so would I.

Before I could send out an email to complain to the toilet paper people, I had to gather more facts. I started another Google search and found that one toilet paper company had already freed the tube. That calmed me down a little, but I still want to be reimbursed for all the years of lost squares. I would send an email out later. For now, I was delighted to know I could buy tube-free toilet paper. I was betting Romeo would be just as excited with the findings as I was. I was ecstatic and sent him a text about the great news.

Me: We are going tube-free, baby!
Romeo: What are you going on about now?
Me: Toilet paper. Down with those fucking tubes!
Romeo: And that matters, why?
Me: Because my lady parts don't need to drip-dry!

After texting Romeo, a customer pulled onto the lot. I hobbled outside as fast as I could with my air cast on. The gentleman browsed around the lot, looking at a few vehicles and finally found his way to me.

"I came here Thursday," he said. "But you were closed."

No "Hello" or "How are you today?" It was obvious that he either didn't like small talk or he didn't have any manners. I gave him the benefit of the doubt.

"Yes, the office is closed on Thursdays," I said.

The man scrunched his nose. "That's weird. I've never heard of any other car lot being closed on Thursdays."

"That's the day I go to a dealer auction and try to buy cars for our lot," I explained.

He turned his head and scanned the lot. "I want to speak to the person in charge."

"That would be me," I said, then smiled.

He turned his head back toward me, then scanned me from head to toe, then back. "I mean the owner."

"That would also be me." My smile was beginning to fade.

He took a deep breath. "I want to talk to the man of this establishment."

Asshole must have been related to Barbie. It took everything in my entire being not to snap my fingers in front of his face and draw a Z-formation in the air and say, "Oh no, you didn't just say that!" But I controlled my building anger. "The man of this establishment is at work."

"I need to know the best cash price he can do on a vehicle," he said, as if I couldn't comprehend what he was talking about.

I gave that disrespecting fucker an awful cash price—he deserved one. I guess he didn't like the price I gave him because he ignored what I said. "I'll come back later, when he's here." He started to walk away.

"Please don't," I mumbled.

He spun around at my words. "What did you say?"

I smiled and said, "I look forward to it."

At lunchtime, I had an appointment with the foot doctor. I had re-injured my foot and was back in the air cast. The doctor told me if the swelling didn't go down faster, he was going to give me an injection into my heel during my next visit. The doctor admitted that the shot would hurt. It was super-nice of him to be so honest. Since we were being honest, I asked him if I could exchange my blue air cast for a pink one. He said they didn't make them in pink. I made a mental note to buy some pink spray paint so Romeo could change the color of my cast.

After leaving the office, I sat in Holly and Googled heel injections. It couldn't be that bad. So I decided to watch a few videos on YouTube about the procedure. If it wasn't for the one person screaming and saying, "It fucking hurts!" I might have been okay about it. It was enough to help me make up my mind: that shit wasn't going to happen to me. I had four weeks to find a miracle.

After arriving home, I had to visit Sir Johnny, again. Going to see Doctors made me want to go pee, too. It was hard to explain that phenomenon. It was quite possible doctors owned stock in toilet paper companies and then scared the pee out of patients to make good on their investments. It was just like the scheme where the cereal companies owned stock in Rubbermaid. Both ideas were plausible.

Then a light bulb exploded in my brain. So I sent Romeo a text message. I liked to mess with his mind while he was at work. It was more fun that way.

Me: I just had a brilliant idea!
Romeo: What now?
Me: I thought we could take a road trip.
Romeo: Where to?
Me: I want to go to the Champion 4 toilet plant.
Romeo: Why?

Me: To do a toilet tour!

Romeo: No.

Me: Wait it gets better! American Standard makes that badass ninja toilet. And guess what?

Romeo: God, why me?

Me: We OWN an American Standard toilet! I bet your snack money we own one of those bad boy Champion models. This is so fucking cool! Do you know why?

Romeo: No.

Me: Because you're at work.

Romeo: So.

Me: So, I'm going to start with some smaller items to get Sir Johnny warmed up and ready for the golf balls. I'll make sure to record the historic event with the snazzy smartphone you bought me. See you when you get home!

When Romeo got home, he went directly to the bathroom. I thought he had to visit Sir Johnny, but he just went in there to flush the toilet. Yeah, I messed with his mind pretty good today. He loved me. Good thing I cooked lasagna.

Romeo went back outside to get his stuff at the same time the jerk who wanted to talk to the "man of this establishment" pulled onto the lot. It was like Asshole was across the street just waiting for Romeo to get home. I didn't want to miss out on what that guy had to say, so I cracked the window open and listened like a nosy neighbor. I was like a silent ninja waiting to strike.

"What's the best you can do on that blue car?" The guy asked Romeo and gestured toward the vehicle.

Romeo told him a price and the man's eyes went wide. I had to hold back a laugh. "Be still, silent ninja," I told myself and held my composure. I didn't want to miss one word of their conversation.

"Your wife gave me a better deal than that!" Asshole huffed and puffed like he was going to blow our house down or something.

Romeo chuckled. "Maybe you should've dealt with her. She runs the lot."

"Guess I need to talk to her then," Asshole said, then looked down.

"I'll go get her for you," Romeo replied.

That's my man. He was totally getting laid tonight.

I closed the window and squealed a little, then started doing a little happy dance in the kitchen and laughed my ass off. After Romeo came inside to tell me everything, which I already knew, I took my sweet time going back outside. I enjoyed watching the monitors and seeing Asshole squirm and pace outside the office door.

I knew what Asshole was going to do before I even reached him. Most cash buyers tried it and this guy was no different. Asshole tried to get me to come down another $500.00.

"What would you say if I brought you crisp 100-dollar bills?"

I didn't hesitate to answer. "I'd say you still owe me $500.00."

I stood my ground and the customer laughed, which shocked me, but I wasn't coming down one more dollar. He insulted me, and if he wanted that car, he was going to pay the price. And that price was the $500.00 I might have come down if he wasn't such an arrogant asshole to me earlier.

It was a steep price to pay for an education in mannerisms, but it was money well spent in my opinion. What this guy didn't understand was that nice people get discounts. He should probably start learning to clip coupons because his attitude was costing him some serious money. He eventually went back to his car and got the rest of the money.

Instead of giving Asshole a 90-day warranty on the car he purchased, I should've given him fifty dollars for a six-month supply of tube-free toilet paper. It would've helped clean up his shitty attitude.

Chapter Seventeen

REPO CIRCUS

I was sitting at my desk, going through some past-due accounts and trying to make a decision. If the accounts weren't brought current, I'd have to ask the customers to return the vehicles or I'd have to order them for repo. I glanced at a paper posted on the wall with a picture of a tow truck above the words, "What's the quickest way to get back on your feet? Miss a car payment."

I did everything I could to avoid ordering a repo. I'd much rather figure out a way for a customer to bring their account current instead of taking their car. I'd make phone calls, send emails and write letters to the customers who were past due, but my efforts were usually wasted. No matter the situation, I was always polite, even if I was upset.

Four accounts were severely past due and they were all in repossession status. I should've ordered them for repo months ago, but I held out hope that the customers would hold true to their word through past conversations or emails. After all, we had written contracts and a business to run.

The first account belonged to a couple that bought several vehicles from us in the past and they were great customers. Sometimes, unexpected things happened and I understood that, but I couldn't let a customer take advantage of our kindness and continue to drive a car without paying for it. I did my normal routine and tried to get in contact with each of them, but I wasn't having any luck.

An hour after I first called, I was shocked when the phone rang and the caller ID showed they'd finally called back. I answered the phone.

"I got your message," a female voice said. "We can't pay the past due payments, so we've decided to return the car."

I expected her to pay at least two payments and work something out to bring her account current, but I never expected her to want to return the car. I gritted my teeth and simply replied, "That's fine. Just return the car to the lot. When you're ready, we'll help you get into another car."

"Well," she began and took a deep breath. "There's a problem with that."

"What do you mean?" I asked.

"A guy we loaned the car to got into a little trouble. So the car was towed and placed in impound."

"How long has it been in impound?" I asked and held my breath hoping it hadn't been too long.

"About two months," She said.

I closed my eyes, took a deep breath and did my best to remain calm. I failed. Instead, I slammed my fist on the desk and yelled down the phone.

"You've got to be fucking shitting me!"

"No, I'm not," she said with a little laughter in her voice. "Also, it's 200 miles away."

"What the fuck?" I yelled, again. "We worked with you so you could keep your car and this is what you do to us? Not only are you behind on your car payments, but now we have to pay to get the car out of impound and have it hauled to us from 200 miles away?"

"Yeah, we thought about paying to get it out and bring it to you, but we don't want to waste the money."

"And you think we do? I'll never sell you a car again."

"I know, but we have to do what's best for us. I'm sure you understand." She clearly had no remorse.

"Customers like you are why businesses go out of business," I said. "I am very disappointed with you." I lowered my voice a notch and asked for more details about the location of the car.

After the customer gave me the information, I abruptly ended the phone call without a "thank you" or "goodbye" then sent Romeo a text message.

Me: I'm ducking done with this car lot!

In my haste to send Romeo a quick message, I didn't realize, until after I had sent the text, that the autocorrect feature changed "fucking" to "ducking". I made a mental note to search Google to find out how to add curse words to my smartphone's dictionary.

I took a few deep breaths, then called Tiny and asked him to contact the impound lot. With my luck and my current attitude, the owner would've doubled the fees.

The second customer I called told me he

had mailed a check over a week ago for the entire amount past due. The check still hadn't arrived. He said he would cancel the check and bring me the cash during his lunch hour that day. At one P.M., I sent him a text and told him to bring the money or the vehicle by close of business. An hour later, he replied to my text.

Customer: They need the money or the car today.
Customer: Sorry, that was meant for my mom. She's trying to help me.

Busted! He never mailed us a check in the first place. I chided myself for even believing the old "check's in the mail" bit. I giggled at the text message and sent a reply with the exact amount past due and reminded him that it could be paid online. Just in case I had to order a repo, I contacted a friend who lived in his town and asked him to do a little recon work to see if the truck was at the address we had on file. I didn't want Tiny to waste his time driving to that town if the customer had moved. Sure enough, the truck was there. An hour later he sent me another text to say that he would be returning the truck to the lot this evening.

A few minutes later Tiny called me back.

"I finally got in touch with the impound yard and boy do I have a story to tell you."

I did a facepalm. "Nothing surprises me anymore. Go on. Tell me."

"Apparently, the guy driving the car parked it at a bank, then walked to Wal-Mart. He was arrested for panhandling. There are about eight loaves of molded bread, packages of lunch meat and other food items in the back seat. The floorboards were full of empty soda cans, food wrappers and cigarette packs. I'd hate to be the one to clean it out. The windshield is broken and they don't have a key, either. So they can't tell me how the car runs or how many miles are on it."

"Well, shit," I said, then wondered what the hell I should do. Tiny managed to work out a deal to get the car out of impound and hauled to us first thing in the morning. I took a chance and hoped for the best, then agreed to the deal.

"I have two more repos for you," I said, then sighed. "I'll fax you the details."

"Have you tried to call the customers, yet?" he asked.

"Yeah," I said. "But I haven't heard from either one of them in over four months. I'm done trying to work with them."

"Send me the fax and I'll get straight on it,"

he said.

After sending the information to Tiny, I decided to go through our list of customers. I made a few phone calls and emailed some friendly payment reminders, too.

A few hours later Tiny pulled onto the lot with one of the vehicles I had faxed to him for pick up and came into the office.

"That woman was crazy," Tiny said, then handed me the key.

"What do you mean?" I asked.

"She cursed me like a dog," he said, then laughed. "She told me that you knew she wasn't working and that she planned to pay it off with her tax refund."

I sat back in my chair and rolled my eyes.

"That's news to me. I haven't heard from her. Besides, I'm not going to let her drive it two more months for free."

"You should've ordered that repo months ago," he said, then wrote me a receipt.

"I know, but I wanted to believe everything she told me. I tried to help her." I then signed a check and handed it to him.

"I know you did," he said. "But some people will lie and take advantage of you."

"Not anymore," I said. "I'm done playing games with people. If a certain truck isn't returned to the lot tonight, I'll be calling you in the morning to pick that up, too."

"Just let me know," Tiny said, "I'm off to locate the other vehicle."

♡   ♡   ♡

Two hours later, Tiny called.

"I seriously hope this guy is telling me the truth about having insurance," he said.

"What do you mean?" I asked.

"The car is sitting in his driveway with part of a telephone pole wedged into the side. It's totaled."

"What the duck?" I said, trying out my turned-over leaf.

"Did you just say, 'What the duck?'" he asked.

"Yeah, it's my new word," I said. "I'm trying not to curse so much."

"Good luck with that," Tiny replied, then laughed. "Your customer claims he hadn't had the time to get the police report and file an insurance claim."

"Something doesn't sound right," I said. "Can you get a rollback and have it hauled to the lot? My luck he'd get an insurance check, not fix the car and still owe us the money. We're better off filing the insurance claim under our lienholder rights. That way we'd get the check and have it repaired or apply it to his account, if it's totaled."

"I sure can. I'll see you soon."

I opened the telephone pole guy's file and called his insurance company. As the lienholder, we had the right to contact the customer's insurance company to verify current coverage on a vehicle.

"That policy was canceled on Monday," the insurance lady said. "And the accident happened the following day. The customer tried to make a claim, but we already had the police report."

"So, the vehicle won't be covered?" I asked, even though it was a dumb question.

"No, it won't be covered," she said. "I can fax you a statement and a copy of the police report if you want it for your records."

"Yes, please do. I'll need it to take him to court," I replied, then gave her our fax number.

"Duck! Duck! Duck!" I yelled after I hung up the phone. Then I called Tiny to fill him in on what I had found out about the insurance.

"Tell that ducking asshole, that we'll never sell him another car again."

"I really don't think he cares," he replied.

"And why is that?"

"Because he has another vehicle sitting in his driveway and the temporary tag has his name on it," he said.

"Then tell him I'll see him in court."

After the vehicle was hauled to the lot, I took several photos with my smartphone and sent one to Romeo along with a text that read, "This day ducking sucks!"

Surprisingly, the telephone pole car started right up and it sounded like a dream. It still had low miles and looked great, except for the telephone pole wedged between the front fender and the passenger side door. I contacted the insurance graveyard, where all wrecked vehicles go, to have it placed in their next salvage yard auction.

I closed the office and kept an eye on the video surveillance monitor while I cooked dinner. An hour later, the "check's in the mail" truck was delivered to the lot. I watched the monitor as a man got out, then walked to a car that pulled in after him and he left. A few minutes later, I received a text message from the customer that said his friend had dropped off the truck and the key was under the floor mat.

I poured a glass of wine and finished cooking dinner. I started to feel bad about yelling at our customer earlier, but I took a few sips of wine and brushed those feelings away. That customer cost us money and didn't feel bad about it at all.

In fifteen years, I'd never had a customer make me so angry that I had lost my temper. Of course, I'd wanted to plenty of times, because some people needed to be chewed out and told the truth. But I'd always held my tongue and been professional about everything. That was the old me. If people could manage their stupidity, then I wouldn't have to manage my anger.

The telephone pole guy didn't care about our business losing money either. It's not like he called and offered to pay for the damages—which he was legally responsible for—or felt so bad that he'd continue to pay us what he owed.

I wasn't sure how I kept my composure and made it through another crazy repo day without pulling my hair out. I must have had some kind of ninja brainpower keeping me temporarily sane.

I took a few more sips of wine and wondered how long it would be before Romeo and I would be able to take a much-needed vacation. Then I thought about how companies offered vacation benefits to their employees. Allowing vacations was how businesses kept people working for them. It was time I demanded some benefits from Romeo.

As we sat down for dinner later that night, I

made my demands.

"I want a week vacation every quarter, or I quit," I said, then took a bite of spaghetti.

"You can't quit," Romeo said, then laughed a little.

"Then fire me," I pleaded.

"Okay. You're fired. But you need to be back to work in the morning."

"Well, duck."

Chapter Eighteen

MY WORK IS NEVER DONE

Thankfully the next day was uneventful. After I closed the business and went home, I noticed a pair of Romeo's jeans on the kitchen table. We have a laundry basket in our bedroom and the laundry room, so it seemed unusual enough to ask about.

"Why are your jeans on the table?" I asked.

Romeo glanced from the television toward me. "For some reason, the tools I carry in my back pocket keep making holes in them."

I held up the jeans and examined the pocket with the hole in it. "You mean the screwdrivers?"

Romeo's attention went right back to

watching the game on television. "Yeah, can you patch it up?"

I folded the jeans and put them back on the table. "Sure," I mumbled. "Because that's the kind of wife I am."

Romeo's request caught me off guard. He knew I wasn't a Domestic Goddess reincarnated as Suzy Homemaker. I could mend a few things, but I had limited skills as a seamstress. I owned a sword hammer and pink tools, but not a golden needle. When I got overwhelmed with housework, it was easy enough to call one of our grown children and bribe them with money to do a few chores for me. I loved our kids and they loved money. It was a win-win.

After Romeo went to bed, my mind went into overdrive. I didn't want to sew just any old patch on his jeans. No, I loved Romeo with all my heart and I wanted him to know just how much my heart swelled with joy every time I thought of him. I wanted him to know I would be there for him if he ever wanted me to sew anything for him again because that's what a loving wife did. When my creative side surfaced, amazing things sometimes happened. I wanted Romeo's jeans to scream, "Look at my new patch!" An idea began to form in the corners of my mind and I went to work patching his jean pocket.

When I was finished with the patch, I admired my work. It was simply beautiful and Romeo would definitely know how much I loved him. So would everyone else for that matter.

I was so anxious to find out if Romeo liked my patchwork, that I nearly woke him up, but I decided to let him sleep. I could hardly wait to find out how much he adored the patch.

Romeo usually got up before the rooster crowed and didn't turn any lights on. He got his clothes ready before going to bed and dressed with a nightlight because he didn't want to wake me up. Romeo was such a wonderful man and I was so lucky to have him. My inner girly voice squealed when I thought about it. I knew he would be so happy with my sewing capabilities that I decided to swap the jeans he laid out to wear with the pair I mended.

The excitement kept me from sleeping, so I decided to stay up late and watch a movie. I enjoyed being an adult sometimes. I could eat candy for breakfast and stay up late because I didn't have a set bedtime. But it wasn't long before I started dozing off and found my way to bed before midnight. So much for staying up late.

195

Early the next morning our home phone rang, then my cell phone rang, then the home phone, then the cell phone. The continuous ringing was annoying enough to wake me up from a wonderful dream. I couldn't remember what the dream was about, but I knew it was good, because I was so involved in the other world that I was sleeping like a log. The ringing didn't even budge Romeo awake. His internal clock must have been telling him it wasn't time for him to get up for work yet.

I didn't recognize the phone number calling, but it could've been a friend or family member. If someone called me that early in the morning, then he or she would expect to hear my sleepy-sexy voice. It was bad enough that I had to halfway open my eyes to find the answer button. It took me a few tries, but I managed to answer.

"Who the hell is this and what do you want?" I tried my best to sound polite, but damn, how nice was I supposed to sound at that time of the morning?

"Hello," a woman's voice said. "I've locked my keys in the car and it's still running. Can you see if you have a spare key?"

I closed my eyes and wondered what this woman was doing at this hour to leave her helpless enough to call me. In my half-asleep state of mind, I concluded that she must be a vampire. Then I wondered if she sparkled, like the vampires did in *Twilight*. I opened my eyes again to glance at the clock on my nightstand. "It's five o'clock in the morning and I'm in bed."

"I have to go to work. What am I supposed to do?"

Damn, she wasn't a sparkly vampire from the *Twilight* story. Total let down. It was too bad really. I wanted to ask her about the location of some muscular werewolves living in Forks, Washington because that's where the book said they lived. I would totally hire one to be a security guard for the car lot. I'd just watch him walk around all day long, without his shirt of course, because werewolves didn't need clothes to stay warm.

"Call a locksmith," I said.

"Locksmiths cost money," she replied. I'd give her that. At least she knew locksmiths weren't free. Good for her. Werewolves must be expensive then too. Either that or she didn't really know any of them.

"I'm going back to sleep," I said in the middle of a yawn.

"I guess the car will run until it's out of gas!" She yelled in my ear.

"Or," I yawned again. "You could call a

locksmith."

Sparkles the Vampire Queen was obviously mad because I wouldn't drag my sleepy-ass out of bed and I didn't give a shit. She wasn't a sparkly vampire who had connections with a hunky werewolf. She also crossed a phone etiquette line. Our home phone number was listed in the phonebook and our cell phone numbers were printed on our business cards, but that didn't mean the business was open 24 hours.

I made a mental note to post a sign in the office. People needed to know that it wasn't okay to call a business owner at five o'clock in the morning or any other time when their business was closed. It was especially important for customers to know that calling a business owner at home was *not* acceptable unless it was pre-approved.

I once contemplated using the "do not disturb" feature on my snazzy smartphone, but if an emergency happened, the call wouldn't come through. So, I decided to continue to live with people—vampires or not—calling me at all hours of the night.

I wasn't asleep for too long before Romeo nudged my arm. "Hey, wake up."

"I'm awake," I grumbled without opening my eyes and pulled the blanket closer to my chin.

"What the hell did you do to my jeans?" Romeo asked.

I opened my eyes and squinted at the glaring light, then noticed a fully dressed Romeo. He was standing next to the bed, slightly turned and pointing toward his ass.

"I patched them," I said.

"You used a big red heart!"

"You don't like it?" I asked in a child's voice.

"No, the guys will tease me."

"You do have a cute ass," I said with a sleepy grin.

"That's not the point," Romeo huffed.

"I'll make you a deal," I said. "Wear the jeans to work or let me flush golf balls down the toilet."

"That's blackmail."

"We're married." I smiled again. "It's a compromise."

"We'll talk about this later," Romeo said. Then he stalked out of the bedroom without turning the light off.

"I love you, too," I yelled, then plopped back down and pulled the covers over my head to shield me from the light. I made a mental note to purchase a lower watt light bulb.

After Romeo left, I couldn't stop laughing. I could hardly wait to find out if he was going to wear the jeans to work or give me his blessing to flush golf balls down our toilet. My creativity rumbled again: I had extra red hearts and I could sew them on all of his jeans.

I decided to get up and make some coffee. After taking a few sips of liquid gold, I posted the photo I took of my Domestic Goddess patchwork on social media. It was important to me to take a poll and ask my lady friends what they thought about my handiwork. I did it for all the women who secretly wanted to sew a heart on their husband's jeans. I took one for the team. But mostly I did it because I thought it would be super funny. Which it totally was, because I was still laughing about it. I was kind of weird that way.

All my friends liked it and some even said the consensus seemed to be that other people were going to do it, too. I might have started a viral heart patch thing. I posted one more comment to my friends.

"This is how fashion trends start! If one day you look at a man's ass and notice a red heart sewn on his back pocket, you'll already know how it got started. You. Are. Welcome."

Before I jumped offline, I searched Amazon for some super cute golf balls. It was best to be prepared, just in case Romeo gave me his blessing to flush some balls. Amazon sold pink balls, purple balls and blue balls too, but I discovered some cuter ones and ordered those instead.

After I opened the lot, I looked through Sparkles' file, curious to know if we had a spare key on file. Nope. We didn't have one. I thought about calling Sparkles at 3AM to give her the bad news, but I was above that. Instead, I dialed Sparkles' phone number and left a message to let her know we didn't have a spare. I hoped she felt bad for waking me up and being so rude. She probably didn't care.

As soon as I hung up the phone, it rang. I answered, then reached for my coffee mug.

"Can I come look at a car?" a man asked.

"Yes," I said, then took a quick sip of coffee. "We're open."

"Can I test-drive it too?"

"Yes, we encourage people to test-drive a vehicle before buying it." Just once, I'd like to say that we don't allow people to test-drive a car unless they buy it first.

I seriously needed to drink another cup of coffee and eat a chocolate donut. The early morning phone call still bugged me. Then I remembered the look on Romeo's face when he pointed to his ass. The thought of Romeo's ass put me in a happy mood and I forgot all about Sparkles the Vampire Queen.

A few hours after lunch, a nice truck rolled onto the lot and parked. Soon a man entered the office and stopped in front of my desk. I smiled and greeted him.

The guy ran his fingers through his hair, then said, "I filed bankruptcy and the bank wants to take my truck."

"Okay," I said, not knowing why he was sharing that bit of information with me. He didn't buy his truck from us, so I was a little confused.

The man cleared his throat. "I only owe about $10,000.00. Can you pay off the bank so I can keep my truck?"

"What?" I gasped.

"I can pay you $200.00 per month," the guy offered.

"I'm sorry, but we don't do that," I replied.

"I can't lose my truck!" the man raised his voice.

"I'm sorry," I said, because I meant it. "But we can't help you."

The guy stepped forward. "No, you don't understand!" He yelled, then slammed his hands down on my desk—more on my side than I was comfortable with—and leaned forward. "I need my truck!"

Oh no, he didn't just do that. My ninja gloves were coming off now. Out of instinct I pushed my chair back about two feet, reached toward my gun and wondered what the hell this man's problem was. He had no reason to take his anger out on me.

Holy cheese balls. I nearly pulled my gun out, but I stilled for a moment and just stared at that crazy-ass. He appeared to be a normal when he arrived, and he acted normal too. But that was before he decided to flip the fuck out.

My guess was that this guy's alien-spliced DNA had malfunctioned. He seriously needed to go see a doctor and get some medication to fix that shit. It was either that or he was just plain crazy. I was going with DNA malfunction. It sounded more plausible.

I stood up like Clint Eastwood in any one of his badass gunslinger movies and my chair hit the wall behind me. The loud sound made an unexpected statement that nearly made me jump. Crazy-ass removed his hands from my desk and took a step back. His reaction let on that he knew he had just screwed up. With my hands balled into fists on my sides, I narrowed my eyes and glared at him, silently daring him to try something. Anything.

I could feel my bitch-attitude crawling inside

me and squirming to be set free. I wanted
to take that asshole down. It was all I could
do to keep from saying, "*Go ahead. Make my
day.*" Instead, I surprised myself and remained
calm. It was remarkable—like ninja stuff. I
squared my shoulders and my voice lowered to
a deeper level. An angry, meaner, Clint Eastwood, make-my-day, level. "The office is now
closed," I said.

"I'm sorry," Crazy-ass said. He turned his
palms up in surrender. "I don't know what
came over me."

"I said. The office. Is. Closed." And without
hesitation, I made my way outside in less than
ten steps, with Crazy-ass following me like
a scared puppy. After I was outside, I turned
and slammed the door so hard the window
should've broken. I was glad it didn't. But my
goal was to be outside, where anyone across
the street, next door, driving or walking by,
could see if anything bad was about to happen.
Even though we had video surveillance inside
the office and on the car lot, I felt better being
outdoors.

I just stared at Crazy-ass. I had no plans of
accepting his apology nor did I want to listen
to another word he had to say. This man was
probably on America's most crazy list and he
made me feel like I was in a hostile situation.

Crazy-ass needed to leave and he needed to leave, now.

Out of nowhere, Crazy-ass opened his arms and took a few steps toward me, "I'm sorry. I didn't mean to act that way." He stepped forward wanting to embrace me with an apologetic hug.

Immediately my hands flew out to stop him and I had to push him back. Again, he messed up. I pointed my finger at him and raised my voice to a scarier level. "Nobody touches me, except my husband!"

"I just want to apologize," he said in an innocent tone.

"You need to leave," I said, then pointed toward the road, "Now!" I should have had my phone out dialing the police.

"Okay, okay. I'll leave." Crazy-ass got in his truck and left. I went back to the office, posted a "Closed Early" sign and left for the rest of the day. Closing early was just one of the perks of being a business owner. I went home, poured a glass of wine and started planning dinner. Welcome to my world.

While I cooked dinner and sipped on a glass of wine, I took a moment to reflect on Crazy-ass and his attitude. The guy was going bankrupt and losing everything. He was desperate. Sure, he briefly scared the ninja-shit out of me and he was way out of line, but somewhere, way deep down inside of me, I felt sorry for him. I knew I had it far better. Sure, I didn't get paid for running the car lot, but at least I could afford to buy red heart patches to sew on Romeo's jeans and drink cheap wine while I cooked dinner.

I was grateful for what we had. When Romeo walked through the door, I wanted to let him know just how much I appreciated him. I grabbed his ass and gave him a long romantic kiss, then whispered sweet promises of a passionate night.

When I finished teasing and groping Romeo, he sniffed the air and stepped toward the stove to take a peek at what I was cooking. Nothing gets in the way of a man's grumbling stomach. "I'd love to have pork chops or ribs for dinner."

"I'm allergic to pork," I said, then started to set the table.

"I'm not," Romeo grinned and leaned against the kitchen counter.

I didn't think Romeo would ask me to do any more patchwork, but asking about pork wasn't out of the question. I rolled my eyes. "If I go on a diet and eat healthy food, then you go on a diet and eat healthy food."

"But that's not fair," Romeo said, then folded his arms across his chest.

"I do it for your health," I said. "You. Are. Welcome.

Chapter Nineteen

♡

CRICKET KILLER

We were blessed to live in a small town, away from the big city full of noise and lights. Our rewards came in small packages. For instance, I enjoyed hearing the sweet sound of a cricket's melody to help me drift off into a peaceful sleep. Most people around there did. Not Romeo, though.

When Romeo and I went to bed, a soft cricket lullaby could barely be heard over the fan. It didn't take me long to fall fast asleep.

At about two in the morning, I heard the sound of water pounding on our bedroom window. I bolted straight up in bed, wondering if there were any tornado warnings in the area. I didn't hear any sirens. I reached out for Romeo, but he was gone. I thought he might be in the living room watching the weather channel. He wasn't there. Romeo was nowhere to be found. I soon realized that the water was only pounding on the one bedroom window. It wasn't raining.

I rushed through the house, looking for Romeo, and noticed the back door was wide open. My heart thumped in my chest. I got dressed as fast as I could, then rushed outside toward the front of the house. I had to step over a long stretched water hose, which was normally coiled up inside the hose reel box.

I peeked around the front corner of our home and my mouth fell open. The vision I witnessed left me curious, worried and just plain baffled. Romeo was outside, in the middle of the night, in a robe and slippers. He was using the powerful jet stream on the water hose and drenching our bedroom window with more water than it took to wash away all the elephant poop on a circus stage.

He didn't know I was there yet, and he was talking. Actually, he was yelling.

"Die, you fucker. Die!"

I thought I'd seen it all. My husband had finally lost his mind. Welcome to the dark side, I thought.

"Romeo! What are you doing?" I said.

Startled, Romeo's water jet stream changed direction for a moment. "This cricket is driving me insane. I can't fucking sleep!"

I chided myself for not having my phone to record this momentous occasion.

"It's the middle of the night. What are people going to think?"

"I don't give a shit what people think," Romeo said. "This cricket is trespassing!"

The cricket was wedged in a crack behind the windowsill and Romeo was attempting to evict it with water. And it worked. Romeo was a cricket killer. That poor cricket would never make that sweet chirping sound again.

"No need to be alarmed, folks," I said as I walked away. "It's just my crazy-ass husband evicting crickets, via water assassination."

I awoke thirsty and groggy and stayed in the kitchen while I finished coughing up a lung. Asthma didn't do my body good. It just pissed me off. I tried to relax in the living room with a warm cup of coffee until the fire in my lungs subsided and I could breathe better.

Romeo got up early enough in the mornings as it was and I didn't like to wake him when my lungs attacked me during my sleep. No point in both of us losing sleep over my asthma. Bad enough we both lost sleep over Romeo's cricket-killing spree. Poor little cricket.

I glanced at the clock. It was barely after six in the morning and I wondered why Romeo's alarm clock hadn't gone off yet. He didn't like being late for work. I crawled back into bed and gently shook him. "Romeo, what time do you have to be to work?"

Romeo bolted straight up in bed and looked around like a zombie, then at the clock. He stilled for a moment before looking at me, then plopped back down on the mattress.

"What day is it?" he asked.

"I don't know."

"It's Saturday," Romeo replied with confidence.

"Are you sure?" I asked.

"Yes, I'm sure," he said.

"Well, I wondered why your alarm didn't go off." I pulled the blankets under my chin and started to drift off to sleep.

I prayed to God that no customers would come on Saturday. On the weekend, I'd sometimes depend on the video cameras and try to do chores in between customers. By the end of the day, I'd be worn out from splitting my attention between house chores and our customers. Being open six days a week, I didn't have much time to cook, and often I was too tired to even bother. There wasn't any opportunity to go visit family or do anything fun. I was lucky to go grocery shopping.

As a result, our home was looking pretty bad. Dishes and laundry were piled up and the house needed a good cleaning.

I awoke at eleven in the morning and immediately panicked, not sure why Romeo didn't wake me. He was probably in the office selling a car and needed my help. In the middle of getting dressed, I heard strange noises, the sound of the washer and dryer running in the laundry room and dishes being clanked together in the kitchen. What the hell?

My sleepy mind wondered if aliens had invaded our home and took pity on me. I would totally allow them to carry on because I had no problem owning up to my messy house. I knew it wasn't our dog. So it had to be aliens.

I crept down the hallway toward the kitchen. If it was an alien cleaning service, I was going to have to search Google for contact information for Area 51 to report them. But if it were really happening, I'd wait until E.T. finished the dishes, because I wouldn't want to be rude or anything. I needed help that bad.

When I peeked around the corner to the kitchen, I saw Romeo—that ruggedly handsome man in all his male finery—loading the dishwasher. Romeo's responsibilities around the house were outdoor chores and I took care of the inside chores. Looking at him, I felt bad because Romeo worked a full-time job all week, like I did.

"You've had it pretty rough lately," he said. "So I thought I'd give you a jump start. Took care of some customers this morning, then I figured I'd handle some chores while it was slow."

He let me sleep in even though he must have been tired. Romeo didn't want me to have another a meltdown. My husband was fucking awesome! Witnessing my man loading the dishwasher was the sexiest thing I'd ever seen in my life. No matter how stressed I felt, he was totally getting laid at the end of the day—if not sooner.

I could say I enjoyed working every Saturday, but I'd be lying. Saturdays weren't evil like Mondays, but they could be very trying.

I was filing some paperwork when a nice couple entered the office and asked about a fully loaded van we had for sale. They had driven over three hours to get to our lot and were eager to take it for a test-drive. Just as

I was handing over the keys, the gentleman wanted to confirm the $1,995.00 on the windshield. "So, that's the price of the van, right?"

"No," I said, then pulled my hand back and gripped the keys in my palm. "That's the down payment."

The guy took a step back. "What do you mean, the down payment?"

"We do on-the-lot financing. That's the down payment. The monthly payment, interest and terms are printed on the form posted inside the window. We also give you a 90-day warranty," I said.

The man looked confused. "What's the full price?" He asked.

I tapped my phone open, pulled up our inventory list and showed him the price as I said, "$7,995.00."

The guy lowered his voice. "That's way too much for that vehicle."

"It's only three years old, with low miles and new tires," I said.

"I'm willing to pay $1,995.00 and that's it," he said.

"Well," I began while putting my phone away. "I'm not willing to accept that." I glanced at our sign to make sure Romeo didn't change the business name to "Let's Make a Deal."

"I know how you car dealers work," he said.

I stepped away from the customer, out of arm's reach, because I couldn't stop my mouth from what it was about to say. "Do you?" I challenged him. "Please, tell me how us car dealers work. Enquiring minds want to know."

"You're all fucking crooks!" he yelled. Then he looked at his wife. "We're leaving."

"Good luck in your search," I said with a chipper tone and raised a hand to wave them goodbye.

I nicknamed that customer Wolf because he huffed and puffed, then stomped away, mumbling the entire way to his car.

As Wolf and his mate were leaving, a truck pulled up and parked near the office door.

Since I was already outside, I lingered around to answer any questions if the new customer had any. Sometimes, people just wanted to browse around and there was no need to bother them.

The customer turned out to be looking for a certain vehicle and had a ton of questions. I directed him inside the office so we could talk. He explained that he was retired military and just wanted straightforward answers. He had cash to buy and didn't need financing. I had no problem with that. Cash customers meant less paperwork to deal with.

Since this guy didn't tell me his name, I

secretly named him General. General wanted a four-wheel drive truck. We had three in stock. The truck had to have four doors. Only one met that criteria. He asked about pricing, mileage and warranties. Then he asked about the price of a crossover vehicle that looked like an SUV. I told him that one was two-wheel drive.

General snarled at me. It's a good thing he didn't growl or I would've had to give him a new nickname. "When I ask you a question, I expect a direct answer."

"I gave you a direct answer. You said you wanted a four-wheel drive and that one is two-wheel drive." I felt my blood pressure begin to rise.

"That's not what I asked!" General leaned forward, then slammed his hands down on my desk. "Are you going to answer me or not?"

At least he kept his hands on the far side of the desk and away from me. What was with people slamming their hands on my desk lately? I wondered if he was related to Cra-zy-ass who was here yesterday. I closed my price book, pushed my chair back and stood to look down at him. I didn't reach for my gun, nor did I feel threatened. This guy was just plain rude and needed to learn a valuable lesson. "It's not for sale," I said.

"What about the truck?" General asked.

"That's not for sale either," I said.

"Is my money not good enough for you?" General demanded.

"No, it's not," I said.

General stood, pulled out his wallet and threw a stack of 100-dollar bills on my desk. "What do you say to that?"

Like cash money was going to impress me and make up for his bad attitude. I wasn't some stripper on a pole. This guy didn't know me at all, but it was time for him to find out. "The office is closed."

General snatched up the money and stormed out of the office. "You're a bitch!"

I followed him just to make sure he found his way out. "You have no idea," I mumbled. Then I said, "Have a nice day."

Once we were both outside, I turned to shut the office door, but I accidentally slammed it instead. I didn't mean to slam the door. It just happened. I blamed high blood pressure, pre-menopause, and the car lot. None of it was my fault.

Before the door slammed shut, I vaguely remembered hearing the chirping sound of a cricket, but I couldn't hear it anymore. It might be stuck in the office and I needed to let it out because it could have a family of crickets and they could be worried about where it was. More importantly, I was married to a cricket killer and I needed to save it from a certain death.

"You didn't have to slam the door!" General yelled as he climbed into his truck.

"Have a nice day," I said, then smiled as I waved him goodbye.

I ignored General as he squealed his tires and burned rubber out of the driveway. So far it was raining stupid today. I made a mental note to search Amazon for a dumbrella.

I opened the office door and noticed a squashed cricket in the doorframe. Now Romeo and I were both cricket killers. The only difference was mine was involuntary insect slaughter. Romeo will never know that I joined him on the list of cricket killers.

Chapter Twenty

I SHOULD GET PAID
FOR MY GENIUS

I had my fill of stupid earlier in the day after dealing with the big bad Wolf and the screaming General. I glanced at the time on my snazzy smart watch, hoping this day would soon end. At that moment, I had an epiphany about wearable technology. People wear things to monitor heart rates, sleep activities and how many steps they take. Technology has the capability of doing so much more. Great innovations are born from great inventions.

I had an idea and it was freaking awesome.

I went into our house and logged onto the computer in our kitchen. Using that computer let me keep an eye on the car lot through the video surveillance at the same time. Romeo drank his coffee while scanning through the television channels to record a sports game or a race or something.

"What's going on?" he asked from the living room.

"I need to send an email to Fitbit."

"Why?" Romeo asked, not that he was really paying attention.

"Fitbit is neglecting the perfect opportunity for mass-market sales."

"What are you going on about now?" Romeo said as he walked into the kitchen.

I stopped what I was doing and turned to face him. "Fitbit has the technology and the obligation to market the most obvious wearable. I can't believe nobody else has thought about it. We could be rich."

"You lost me," Romeo said, then poured another cup of coffee.

"Fitbit needs to make a wearable to track stupid people, but it's not for the person wearing it. No, it's for normal people, like me, to recognize when a person has reached their maximum stupidity for the day," I explained. "It could notify the user that they need to rest or take a pill or something. They could call it the Stupidbit."

Romeo laughed. "You've lost your mind."

"No, stupid people have," I said. "They should be required to wear the Stupidbit for the safety and continued sanity of normal people."

Romeo coughed to cover up a laugh. "You're not normal," he said.

I ignored him. "The Stupidbit could monitor the user's vital signs and it could change colors during different levels of stupidity. You know, like a mood ring. It's perfect!"

I sent an email to Fitbit explaining the details of my awesome idea. At the end of the email, I told them I personally knew someone who could do the marketing campaign for the Stupidbit and she wasn't stupid. I supplied them with all my contact information, including my phone number. They could have their people get in touch with my people. Or they could simply send me an email and I'd take care of it, but first I'd need compensation.

I poured another cup of coffee and my mind was still reeling from the stupid I had dealt with that morning. Then it hit me. Damn, I was on a roll today. I turned back to the computer and reached out to my dear friend Google. Google was the smartest friend I had.

I started searching for information about how to start a television network or cable channel. I wasn't exactly sure what I was looking for. I just knew when there was a need for something, it should be made available to the public. And I was here for the public. I could run for president!

"What are you doing now?" Romeo asked.

"I'm sending an email to HBO and Netflix."

"Why?"

Romeo just didn't understand sometimes. I was doing important research. I took a deep breath and mimicked Romeo's favorite position and leaned against the counter. I then took a sip of coffee before I answered him. "I have an idea for a cable or television show. If HBO doesn't want it, then maybe Netflix will."

Romeo raised his eyebrows, "What's in your coffee?"

I rolled my eyes. "Just like Fitbit, HBO and Netflix have neglected an opportunity to get in on this action. So it's up to me to do something about it."

"Do something about what?" Romeo asked, then flipped through the newspaper.

"My television show idea," I said. "Aren't you listening?"

Romeo reluctantly stopped reading the sports section and looked up at me. "Okay, I'm listening. What would you call your television show?"

I smiled, finally getting his full attention. "WTF television. It would stream stupid 24 hours."

"That's stupid," Romeo replied, then closed the newspaper.

"You finally understand," I said.

While I was finishing up my Google research and putting together an email draft, Romeo collected a package from the UPS driver. "Something came for you."

I turned away from the computer. "Me? Cool beans! I love surprises."

He handed me the box, "You don't know what you ordered?"

"I can't remember. But I bet it's super-awesome!"

It was a package from Amazon with a big smile on it. Just seeing that logo made me all happy inside. Our world needed more of that. Kudos to Amazon for spreading smiles worldwide.

Romeo stood on the other side of the kitchen table curious to see what arrived. "What is it?"

I cut the packing tape and a giggle escaped my mouth as I opened the box. I reached in, then pulled the item out and gazed at it for a moment. I nearly cried with joy. It was the most amazing thing Amazon sold on their website, aside from books. In my hands was a twelve-pack box of golf balls I had ordered a few days ago. I turned it around and held it out toward Romeo with both hands, so he could see it full view, but not take it away from me.

"What the fuck?" Romeo said.

"Isn't it awesome?" I squealed.

"No," Romeo said flatly.

I turned the package back toward me, then hugged it with delight. These weren't just any golf balls. No, these were super special. The clear plastic front of the package revealed bright yellow golf balls with different happy emoji expressions on each one of them. They'd look so cute and happy swirling around in Sir Jonny's cold pool of water.

I wasn't sure if it was my excitement or too much coffee, but I needed to visit Sir Johnny, and fast. So I took off sprinting down the hall-way toward the bathroom with a big smile on my face.

"Where are you going?" Romeo asked.

"To the bathroom," I called over my shoulder with glee.

"What are you going to do in there?"

I stopped in my tracks and turned back toward Romeo. If I wanted to play this off correctly, I'd need to feign perfect innocence. As my hands tightened around the box I held, I glanced down at the peppy emoji balls. What kind of wife would I be if I passed up the perfect chance to mess with him? Not a very good one. He'd given me such a hard time about wanting that toilet, and I'd wanted to pay him back for that almost as much as I wanted to flush the golf balls for real.

"Did you just ask what I'm going to *do* in the bathroom?"

"With you, it's a legitimate question," Romeo said.

Romeo was going down. My crazy gloves were coming off now. I tried my best, but I couldn't hide my mischievous grin. "Do golf balls float?"

"Why do you ask?" Romeo said. I could hear the panic in his voice.

"Never mind," I said. "I'll find out." I turned away and ducked into the bathroom, then locked the door and started laughing like a lunatic. I flushed Sir Johnny three times, spacing the flushes out and giving the tank time to refill. Between flushes I'd yell, "That's one! Two! Three strikes you're out!" I knew I was playing with golf balls, but "Take Me Out to the Ballgame" came to mind and I couldn't resist. Besides, I didn't know any cute toilet tunes so the baseball song it was.

Before I could flush Sir Johnny a fourth time, I heard a knock on the bathroom door. It was all I could do to keep from really laughing because we had a second bathroom and there was no need for Romeo to interrupt my precious bathroom time.

"Who is it?" I asked, as if I didn't know.

"What are you doing in there?" Romeo's voice penetrated the walls of the throne room.

"What do you think I'm doing in here?" I continued to laugh and with each flush, I talked more crazy-talk. "Now, which one of you adorable balls is going down next?"

I must have been in there for at least ten minutes. Finally, I washed my hands and opened the bathroom door to find Romeo leaning against the hall wall with his arms crossed against his chest. He glared at me over his glasses and gave me that you're-in-trouble-now look. I wasn't sure which was funnier, Romeo waiting outside the bathroom for ten minutes or the look he gave me. I kept my laughter in check and grinned again. "Sorry, did you have to use the bathroom, too?"

"What did you do in there?" Romeo demanded.

"What do normal people do in a bathroom?"

"You're not normal," Romeo said.

I placed a hand over my heart. "That hurts."

Our water bill might be a little higher this month, but it was so worth it just to see the uncertainty on Romeo's face. I scooped up the happy emoji golf balls, intent on hiding them and strolled past Romeo with my chin held high.

I knew just the place to stash the emoji balls. The room I took over after our last child left the nest was now my Woman's Cave. I filled it with my favorite books and exercise equipment that rarely got used. It was my quiet place.

I glanced over at a section of books and smiled. Hidden behind those glorious tomes were my diabolical Elf on the Shelf items. Our kids were all grown up and moved out now, so I could do whatever I wanted to do without needing to worry about their precious minds being corrupted. Romeo had no idea what was in store for him leading up to Christmas. December was going to be awesome.

I pulled a section of romance books toward the front of the shelf, then removed the golf balls from the package and scattered them behind the books. Romeo was a certified cricket killer, but I wouldn't put it past him to smash my balls.

Chapter Twenty-One

♡

EVIL MONDAY STRIKES BACK

Coffee is what I needed to function in the morning. Coffee cleared my mind and gave me a little taste of heaven before entering Monday hell. I always had high hopes for Monday, but often something happened to let me down. It was best to be prepared with coffee in the morning and wine in the evening. It helped to balance things out.

The only way to start a Monday off poorly was not having any coffee. And I was out of coffee. Shit!

I had plenty of time before I had to open the car lot, so I snatched up my keys and purse, then rushed outside only to be met with a blast of cold air. It was so cold I went back inside and grabbed a jacket, then jumped in Holly and raced to the grocery store. Before I went inside, I used my smartphone and checked the local weather. The temperature was already freezer-cold and a snow blizzard was coming our way. I was hoping I could close the office early. I was so excited that I checked the weather in Orlando, Florida, then took a screenshot of the forecast and texted it to Romeo. I was betting he'd like to know that it was warm and sunny somewhere. He'd thank me later.

I turned down the coffee aisle and scanned the shelves for my favorite unleaded Folgers coffee. If I drank caffeinated coffee, I'd be bouncing off the walls until lunchtime. No thank you, caffeine.

I looked and looked, but my favorite coffee wasn't to be found. I started to panic, took a deep breath, and remained calm. There were plenty of decaffeinated Folgers coffees on the shelves, but I preferred to buy the box with single pack servings. I scanned the aisle and asked the first employee I found if the store had any of my coffee in the stockroom.

I paced along the coffee-scented aisle enjoying the intoxicating aroma in the air. When the worker returned, he informed me that the store no longer stocked it. It was nice of him to suggest that I could buy a jar of instant coffee or I could possibly buy the single serving packs online. *What the hell?* The store had plenty of single regular coffee packs, but they didn't stock the unleaded. It wasn't fair. It was an outrage. It was coffee discrimination. I needed to find a good lawyer. But first, I needed coffee.

Reluctantly, I went to the checkout lane to pay for a jar of instant coffee. The adorable cashier lady, about half my age, greeted me with a smile. Then she asked me in a perky morning voice if I had found everything I was looking for. She obviously had her coffee choice this morning. I simply said, "No." She looked a bit surprised, probably not expecting that kind of grouchy answer, and I didn't care to elaborate. If I ever saw that perky cashier again, I would apologize for my rude behavior. I blamed a lack of coffee, pre-menopause and the car lot.

After I got home, I searched Google and found the grocery store's corporate phone number and called them. Apparently, it was a marketing decision to discontinue selling that item in their store due to poor sales in our area. I didn't understand how the store could have low sales when I bought it all the time. It made no sense. I pretended to be okay with the explanation, even though I wasn't. My opinion clearly didn't matter. Frustrated, I hung up the phone only to receive a text message.

Romeo: Why did you send me that?
Me: I wanted you to feel all warm and fuzzy inside.
Romeo: I don't give a damn about Florida!
Me: No coffee, huh?

If I had known we were out of coffee, I would have been more sensitive to how I communicated with him. I wouldn't have written him a heartfelt note, sealed it in a pink envelope and placed it inside Romeo's lunch box last night with strict instructions not to open it until his first break. There was nothing sweeter than reading a love letter on first break and being surrounded by close friends.

I'd used a regular sheet of copy paper and printed a photo of his heart patch jeans. It was the perfect background to help support my romantic thoughts. I'd even gone so far as loading my lips with bright red lipstick and kissed the paper at the bottom, just below Romeo's left butt cheek. It was absolutely adorable.

I thought it might brighten Romeo's day. But now that I had more time to think about it, he might not like it very much. He'd only laugh if he was in the mood for that. Without coffee? Maybe a more hostile reaction.

I had envisioned Romeo picking up the pink envelope, bringing it toward his nose to smell the sweet scent of my favorite perfume, then waving it toward his friends in the cafeteria, who would no doubt be gawking at him in awe.

Romeo wouldn't stop there. No, he'd say something like, "Jealous? You should be," then fist-bump a friend next to him and say, "I'm getting laid tonight!"

But now I could picture the next step. Romeo would then take his time opening the envelope like a delicate flower and his face would beam like rays of sunshine as he began to read my loving words. Within seconds his smile would fade away and he would read my love letter again and again. His hands would start to tremble as panic invaded his mind.

Romeo would drop the letter and start twisting around from side to side to try and view his ass and feel both pockets to see if I had switched his jeans again. His friends might wonder what was wrong with him.

It wasn't like Romeo would actually stand up and ask his friends if there was something on his ass. I only knew a few women to do that sort of thing, including me. I have no shame.

Romeo's friend, next to him, would pick up the romantic letter and read it out loud.

"Dearest Romeo, I love your ass. I'm sure everyone else is admiring it today too. Have a wonderful day!"

I tried to shake off that image and focus. The tough thing about buying coffee online is that it required focus, which for me required coffee. If I could get this taken care of now, I could at least prevent further disasters.

I turned to Amazon to find my coffee and did a search for Folgers single coffee packets and noticed only two pages came up. No way was I going to buy the first one at the top of the list because there were different size boxes on Amazon and I wanted to buy bulk at a good price. I finished scanning through the first page, then clicked next to go to the second page and what I saw left me speechless.

The second page only listed one item and the description read: Coffee Enema Starter Kit. I wasn't sure why someone would want to waste perfectly good coffee and squirt it up his or her ass. I was floored. I couldn't believe what I was reading.

The Coffee Enema Starter Kit included three packs of generic single brew coffee packs, one blue enema bulb and three packs of lubricant.

Strange, I've only watched commercials on television showing people drinking the coffee. This coffee kit looked like it was more for friends with special benefits. Not that I'd want to see an advertisement for coffee squirting enemas.

I wasn't interested in the coffee enema, at least not that morning. But I was happy with my instant cup of coffee in hand, so I continued to read. I laughed so hard coffee was squirting out my nose. At least it wasn't coming out of my ass. Flushing golf balls are my kind of thing, not coffee enemas.

At noon the local news announced schools were shutting down and urged all businesses to close early to allow employees to leave and prepare for the incoming winter storm. Newscasters should just say, "Go to the grocery store and buy all the milk and bread you can." It was the same thing. The news also warned people to stay off the roads once the storm hit, unless it was an absolute emergency.

By the time Romeo arrived home, the blizzard was in full force and I was busy making a big pot of chili. As he came in the door, a customer pulled into the lot. I then noticed I had forgotten to turn off the 'open' sign. I blamed the snow.

As I walked toward the office to close up and turn the lights off, the customer stopped me and asked if he could test-drive one of our sports cars. The wind was howling and a snowplow drove past our lot. I wondered if I had heard him correctly. Mother Nature had put me in a bad position once before when I didn't hear what a customer had said because of the wind. I didn't want to make that mistake again.

I wiped the fallen snow away from my face. "You want to test-drive a car in this weather?"

"Yeah, work let me off early because of the storm, so I had the time."

"A four-wheel drive can barely make it through this snow, let alone a Mustang," I said and pointed toward the slow moving traffic.

"I know how to drive," he began. "And I have insurance, too."

I pushed some snow aside with my boot. "There's ice under that snow and our insurance doesn't allow test-drives during these weather conditions."

Just as the words left my mouth, the garage door opened and Romeo drove the tractor out so he could get a head start on the plowing. The wind was howling and the snow was coming down so fast that the customer was starting to resemble Santa Clause. His hair and beard were covered in snow. All he needed was the red suit. Santa chose to ignore what I had said and took that opportunity to approach Romeo. The wind kicked up a notch and I only caught part of their conversation.

Romeo lifted his hat away from his ear and leaned forward. "You want to do what?"

Santa cupped his hands around his mouth and said, "I want to drive the Mustang sleigh in the snow." Maybe I heard him wrong, but that was what it sounded like to me.

Romeo shook his head. "Are you crazy?"

Reluctantly, Romeo ended up taking Santa for a ride in the Mustang sleigh. Santa's driving privileges had been revoked and his cheeks were rosy red, clearly not happy about being in the passenger seat. Santa apparently didn't know that an eight-cylinder rear-wheel drive wasn't the same as eight flying reindeer. I guess when you only drive reindeer that's a mistake you could easily make.

After what seemed like an hour, Romeo slid back onto the driveway and parked the Mustang sleigh. Santa got out and followed Romeo into the office to place the vehicle on hold until the weather cleared up.

Santa waved his hands over the heater, then looked at Romeo as he started the paperwork. "I've never bought a car that I didn't actually test-drive."

Romeo didn't even bother to look at him. "I've never had a customer ask to test-drive a car during a blizzard."

Santa stood a little straighter, then tucked his hands in his coat pockets. "I can't be the first one."

"Yes, you are."

After Santa left, Romeo got back on the tractor to finish what he hadn't started. I was as happy as a little girl watching Romeo plow the driveway. This blizzard would cripple our town for the next few days—if not more—and that meant I didn't have to work. I got to use a snow day and that meant I didn't have to deal with any customers. Yay! Thoughts of the hot chili simmering on the stove made me feel warm and fuzzy and I began thinking of things I could do to keep me busy. Like building a family of snowmen and using Romeo's summer clothes. I was going to have so much fun.

The blizzard was relentless and Romeo couldn't keep up. I wanted to help, so I started shoveling the sidewalk and between the cars. My damn lungs started to burn, which made me cough so hard it was taking me longer to shovel than I expected. Stupid lungs! Stupid asthma!

On the plus side, I looked super cute wearing my purple hat. The hat was made to resemble some goofy looking animal and it had long braided ears to tie under my chin, but they looked cute just dangling. The moment I laid eyes on that hat, I knew it was made specifically for me—and maybe for the kid who had been in the middle of asking his mom to buy it for him. I snatched it up before Mommy got a chance to look at it. Snooze you lose!

Romeo would plow one section of snow and finish another area, then look back to find the previous section already covered again. He must have been listening to rap music through his earbuds because every once in awhile I'd hear Romeo sing a few words when he glanced around to look at the snow covered drive. "Motherfucker! Hell no. I plowed that shit!"

It was time Romeo heard an adorably cute song so he could be as happy as I was. I marched through the snow and waved my arms above my head to get Romeo's attention. He then idled the tractor down to a lower decibel so he could hear me.

I then belted out a happy tune about building a snowman, one that would stay on his mind and take at least four days before he could forget it. If it weren't for our precious grandchildren watching the children's movie *Frozen* over and over when they came to visit, I wouldn't even know the words. They'd be so proud of me.

"Let's go play!" I yelled, then twirled around like a ballerina.

I continued to twirl, but Romeo rolled his eyes and took off on the tractor. The happy song and ballerina moves must have worked because I didn't hear him sing any more rap for the rest of the time he was plowing.

The blizzard finally won and Romeo decided to finish plowing the snow in the morning, before going to work. Poor Romeo didn't get snow days, but I did. I had huge plans. Sleeping late, drinking coffee, staying in my pajamas all day and reading a book came to mind. Tomorrow was going to be the best snow day ever. I didn't even have to cook dinner because I had just made a huge pot of chili. Leftovers usually lasted a few days.

"You thought your love note was cute, huh?" Romeo said as he crushed crackers and sprinkled them on top of his chili.

I nearly choked from laughter. I'd briefly forgot about the romantic note I placed in Romeo's lunchbox. "I like to keep you on your toes," I said. "So, did you like it?"

"No."

"Not even a little?"

"No."

"I'll do better next time," I beamed.

"No more love notes, Julia."

"You take the fun out of everything."

Romeo just grinned as he reached for the peanut butter. "You know it can be really embarrassing when people at your place of work see that kind of stuff."

He had taken out his phone and was fidgeting with it as he talked to me. Something about that smile of his made me nervous.

He turned the phone around to show me. It was our car lot's Facebook page. On top, a new video had been uploaded. It already had hundreds of views and likes.

"I took a moment to return the favor," he said.

"Oh no."

I winced and pressed play on the video. It was security footage of our lot this evening. Romeo had edited together shots me of dancing with the broom and twirling around the cars. At the time, it had just been a fun thing to do before my asthma kicked in. Now I just looked like someone who needed to be locked up. At least the caption was sweet: "My snow angel, the dancing queen."

I instinctively pushed the phone back to

Romeo.

"Okay, I get it. I'm sorry."

"We're even," he said. "I'll take it down now."

Romeo had gotten me back and then some. It didn't matter if he took it down, the damage was done. I pouted dramatically, but part of me had to admit he'd gotten me good.

"Okay, no more pranks," he said. "Let's get to the good stuff: your birthday is coming up. Any idea what you want?"

My eyes shot up. "A new toilet and a ton of golf balls."

"There's nothing wrong with our toilet," Romeo said before taking a bite.

"Sir Johnny needs an upgrade," I said.

"No," he said, then scooped another spoonful of chili into his mouth.

"I think I'll patch a few more of your jeans tonight," I retorted with a grin.

The next morning Romeo plowed the driveway and shoveled a path from our house to the office door. He took a photo with his phone, texted it to me, then posted it on social media along with one sentence, "The office is open."

Well, shit.

Chapter Twenty-Two

♡

I'M OKAY

During the snowstorm that disabled our town for a few days, I thought I'd get caught up on paperwork, but that wasn't the case. Nobody actually came to the office because of the weather, but the phone rang off the hook. At one point I received three voicemail messages during one phone call. And while I returned the missed calls, I received more missed calls and additional voicemail messages. It was a long two days.

Finally the roads cleared up and more people were out and about, but the weather was still frigid. Jack Frost was having the time of his life that winter. I dressed in warm winter apparel, then armed myself with the kitchen broom and went to the lot with intentions of clearing the snow off all the vehicles. It was going to take a while with so much snow.

As I approached the vehicles on the front row, I figured out what Romeo was doing and why it took him a little longer spreading salt on the driveway again last night. Romeo had drawn happy, sad or crazy faces in the snow on each car windshield. His snow art was totally cute and funny at the same time. He certainly knew how to make me smile and quite possibly the motorists passing our lot would smile too. I pulled my phone out and took a few photos to upload them to social media later that night.

By the time I cleared the snow off the second car, my breathing became a chore and my lungs were on fire. I was born to live on a beach somewhere in a warmer climate. This snow was for the birds. Well, not actually the birds, because they flew south for the winter and stayed warm in a tropical climate, while I was stuck here suffering through these blasted cold months.

By around lunchtime, my hands and feet were frozen and I couldn't feel my toes. I continued working until I brushed the snow off the last vehicle. As I began walking back toward the office, a customer pulled onto the lot.

The gentleman approached me and asked about the prices on a few of the four-wheel drive sports utility vehicles and wanted to know more about the warranties we offered.

"Let's go inside where it's warmer," I said.

"Are you sure?" he asked, which I thought was kind of an odd question.

"Yes, I'm sure," I said. "It's freezing out here."

The customer followed me inside and I nodded toward a seat across from my desk, then I walked over to the gas heater and placed my hands over the flames to get some feeling back into my fingers. After the tingling sensation went away, I took the seat behind my desk and we talked more about pricing and warranties.

The customer glanced down at the zipper on his coat a few times and I started to feel bad for having the heater set on high. Just because I was freezing from being outside for so long didn't mean he was too. "If it's too hot in here, I can turn the heat down," I offered.

"No," the man said. "I'm fine, thank you."

The customer wanted me to write down the prices on the back of our business card because he had just started his search to buy a new vehicle. I reached for a card and noticed that the customer was wearing a yellow scarf tucked inside his black coat. Again, he glanced down at his zipper and I wondered if he was self-conscious about wearing a yellow scarf in public. Why in the world would I care what color scarf he was wearing? I was wearing a bright pink scarf with matching gloves and a silly purple hat that screamed adult-child and it didn't bother me.

I finished writing the information on the back of the card and slid it across my desk toward the customer. As he leaned forward and reached for the card I heard a hissing sound. Then I noticed something slither out of his coat, just above his zipper and face me. It hissed again.

Oh, my goddess. He had a snake in his jacket. I stood up so fast my chair hit the back wall with a loud crunch. It probably cracked the drywall, but I didn't give a shit. I stumbled backward trying my best not to fall or trip over anything behind me, then pointed an accusing finger toward the man and his slithering friend.

"What the fuck?"

"You said you didn't mind if I came inside," Snake Man said, like it was not a big deal.

"I didn't know you had a snake in your coat," I said, not taking my eyes off him.

"He's harmless," Snake Man said, as he pulled his yellow friend out of his coat. He then stood up and began to stretch his arms out toward me.

Did he really think I wanted to hold it? Just because he liked snakes didn't mean anyone else did, especially me. I stepped out from behind my desk and made my way toward the exit and started screaming like a crazy woman. "Keep that thing away from me!"

I ran all the way out to the center of the car lot passing Snake Man's car and started pacing around in circles. I had the sudden urge to pat my coat down, just in case he had another snake and it had gotten loose and crawled up inside my coat without me knowing about it. I just knew I was going to have nightmares after this shit.

Snake Man walked toward his car but didn't give me any indication that he was leaving. He was calm and I was frantic. He probably thought I was a crazed lunatic, but I was thinking the same about him. We stood about thirty feet apart and he still wanted to talk to me.

"I can come back later," he suggested.

"Not with that snake you won't."

Snake Man shrugged, then eased into his car and finally drove away. I kept thinking about that snake slithering its way out of Snake Man's coat. I unzipped my own coat, jerked it off, threw it on the ground, then stomped all over it, just in case. I started pacing around the lot and continued to eye my coat, watching for any unexpected movement. I shivered again from the thought of Snake Man and the yellow slithering friend around his neck, then threw my pink scarf on the ground next to my coat.

I told myself to think happy thoughts and started chanting them out loud over and over: "Romeo cooking dinner. Romeo cleaning the house. Romeo naked. Dinner. House. Naked." It didn't work.

I must have looked like I'd lost my mind pacing around the lot without a coat in those freezing temperatures. Jack, the owner of the *No Crack Plumbing* business across the street made his way toward me. The thought of Jack video taping my crazy coat tantrum and it going viral had me a little worried, but not as worried as I was about a stray snake inside my coat. Jack approached and kept his distance about fifteen feet away from me.

"You okay?" he called out.

"I'm okay," I said. I continued to pace around my coat.

"You don't look okay."

I stopped pacing for a moment to look at Jack.

"A man with a snake was in my office."

"Okay, that explains it."

"I'm just a little freaked out, okay," I said. I definitely wasn't okay. Tears filled my eyes and I swiped them away before they could fall or freeze on my face.

"Okay," Jack replied with a calm tone. He watched as I continued to pace around my snow-covered coat, shaking my arms and trying my best to calm down.

My labored breathing turned into a wheeze as I fought off an asthma attack. The freezing temperatures didn't help my lungs any. I had the heebie-jeebies and my mind was going to be fucked up for the rest of the day. Possibly for the rest of the week or the month, maybe even a year or more. Screw trying to save our insurance company money, I was going to need a lot of professional therapy and possibly medication after that snake.

I paced the lot for another few minutes and finally started to calm down. Jack was on the phone the whole time, probably talking to his partner across the street just in case I needed an ambulance or a straightjacket or something. I settled down and thanked Jack for watching over me during my freak-out session.

After some scrutiny, I made my way toward our house, dragging my coat and scarf on the ground behind me. I still didn't trust that something wasn't slithering inside of it. I let the coat and scarf fall to the ground just outside the door and left them there. No way was I going to take a chance and bring them inside.

I'd have Romeo inspect my coat when he got home. Avoiding the inhaler, I turned the electric kettle on and made myself a hot cup of coffee. I found ways around not using my inhaler, but sometimes it was inevitable.

After my breathing was at an acceptable level, I closed the office for the rest of the day. I needed the rest of the day just to calm down.

I opened a bottle of wine and began making a big pot of vegetable soup. Romeo arrived home about a half bottle of wine later. "Why is your coat on the ground outside?" He asked coming through the door.

"I had a bad day," I said, then took a sip of wine.

"You had a bad day? I bet mine was worse."

"How many chores do you want to bet?" I challenged as I stirred the pot of soup.

"I'll wash the dishes if I lose."

I laughed at that. "You mean you'll load the dishwasher?"

"Yeah, that," he said, then grinned.

"Deal. You go first." I leaned against the kitchen counter.

"One of the new guys that the shop sent to work with my crew arrived early this morning," Romeo began. "Later I found out he only came to work to get his tools. He walked off the job and didn't tell anyone he was leaving, including me. And I'm the boss."

"What did you do?"

"I called his cell phone," Romeo said. "And believe it or not, he actually answered. It must be my older age or something, because ten years ago I would've let the shop handle it."

"What did you say?"

"I asked him why he left without telling anyone. And he said it wasn't the job for him. So I told him he could've at least told someone instead of just leaving. He just said, 'Yeah, I guess I should have.' So I had to call the shop and tell them what happened and to send me another electrician." Romeo had finished his story, then grinned. "I told you I had a bad day."

"You're right," I agreed. "You did have a bad day."

There was no disputing that Romeo had had a bad day. Industrial Electricians were in high demand, and he needed experienced help. I completely understood why Romeo was so upset and I would have been too in his situation. Romeo had to oversee an entire crew. He instructed them on what jobs needed to be done and kept up with their daily hours to make sure they were paid correctly. Romeo's job could be stressful at times, but he enjoyed his profession and had for the past twenty-five years.

"So that means I don't have to do the dishes," Romeo said, ready to celebrate before hearing about my day.

"Not so fast, Romeo Karr," I said, then took another sip of wine. "It's my turn."

I took my time and told Romeo about my encounter with Snake Man. I had no shame when I told him about the plumber watching over me during my freak-out session and why my coat and scarf were outside on the ground.

When I was finished with my story, I poured Romeo a glass of wine and refilled mine. Instead of Romeo replying right away, he sipped his wine and stirred the pot of simmering vegetable soup, then chose his words very carefully. "I'll cook dinner and do the dishes for the rest of the week."

"That's what I thought," I said.

After dinner, Romeo kept his word. He loaded the dishwasher and placed the leftover pot of vegetable soup inside the refrigerator.

He then went to the hall closet, pulled out another one of my winter coats and draped it over another kitchen chair for me to use the next day. "Your coat can stay outside for the rest of the night."

The next morning, when I put on the coat Romeo had left out for me, I noticed it had a heart patch safety-pinned on the front pocket, and I giggled.

Romeo so got me. God, I love that man.

Chapter Twenty-Three

MOVING DAYS

The worst things about Saturday, I couldn't sleep late because we had a business to run and I had to wait four very long hours before I could close. The best things about Saturday: coffee with fresh-from-the-bakery chocolate donuts that melted in my mouth, and having Romeo home to share the workload of the car lot.

With a cup of coffee in one hand and my second chocolate donut in the other, I dragged my feet toward the office. Moments after opening, the phone rang to start my workday.

"Do you rent vehicles?" a woman asked.

"Sorry, we're not a rental company. Our insurance doesn't allow that."

Gazing out the window, I sipped my coffee and watched Romeo pour a gallon of gasoline into a few vehicles. After a test-drive or two, we had to put more gas in them. Not having a full tank of gas deterred customers from taking an extended joy ride. And in theory, if a vehicle was stolen, the car thief wouldn't get far before needing to find a gas station.

A motorcycle with an exhaust system loud enough to rattle the windows pulled onto the lot. The rider came into the office and introduced himself.

"I'd like to test-drive a few of your trucks," he said. "I'll start with the long bed."

I handed Rider a test-drive form, copied his driver's license and slid the truck keys into my pocket. When he was done, I tucked a magnetic dealer plate under my arm, then picked up the jump-box and walked Rider to the truck. I handed the key over and asked the customer to start the truck. As soon as the truck started, I set the jump-box aside and attached the dealer plate to the tailgate. Satisfied that the plate was secure and wouldn't shake off during the drive, I reminded Rider—per the test-drive sheet—that test-drives are only fifteen minutes.

After he left, I picked up the jump-box and headed back toward the office. Romeo had pulled out the 35-gallon gas tank and various size jugs to load them on the back of his truck. "We're out of gas," he said. "I need to take these and fill them up."

"And I need another donut," I giggled, but Romeo didn't laugh. He probably needed more coffee. "But I'll help you load them."

After Romeo left, I licked my lips in anticipation of eating another melt-in-your-mouth chocolate donut and made my way toward the house. When I opened the box, it was empty. Romeo ate the last donut! He didn't know the meaning of 50/50. I hadn't had enough chocolate this morning so I made a cup of mocha cappuccino.

As I was taking a sip of chocolate heaven, my phone rang. It was Romeo. So I answered, "You ate the last donut!"

"Listen," Romeo said. "The guy who is test-driving the truck isn't test-driving it."

"What do you mean, he *isn't* test-driving it?" I asked and glanced at my watch. Rider had already been gone 25 minutes. Shit. I lost track of time helping Romeo load the gas tank and jugs.

"He's moving furniture with it!" Romeo yelled through the phone. "I passed him on the way to the gas station and now I'm following him. You need to meet me."

"Okay," I said, then snatched my keys and ran out the door.

Romeo stayed on the phone and gave me directions to where he was until I spotted his truck and pulled in behind him. Romeo didn't want Rider to know we were there, so we remained in our vehicles.

A few houses down I observed the test-drive truck backed into a driveway and watched Rider unload furniture with the help of a woman. I'd bet some chocolate donut holes that she was the same woman who called and asked if we rented vehicles.

I took some photos for proof. I was doing important ninja surveillance.

"Do you want me to call the police?" I asked Romeo on the phone.

"No," Romeo said. "I have something better in mind."

As Rider and the woman were hauling the last mattress inside, Romeo stepped out of his vehicle, then jogged to the test-drive truck. I didn't utter a word and held my breath as Romeo eased the door open, climbed in, started it up and pulled out of the driveway. Damn! He was doing badass ninja stuff. We were so made for each other.

Romeo sped away and I followed him back to the lot.

"You were lucky the key was in the ignition," I said.

"Yeah, but I was prepared to confront him to get the key and make him walk back to get his motorcycle," he said. "I wasn't about to let him drive the truck again or give him a ride."

After we returned to the lot, Romeo worked on a few things outside, but he stayed close to the office. He didn't want Rider coming to get his motorcycle without an explanation.

Thirty minutes later I received a call from the local police department. Rider called and reported the truck stolen. He told the police he had stopped at a friends' house to show her the vehicle. When they walked outside it was gone. The officer wanted us to meet him at the address it was stolen from to get a full report.

As we approached Rider and the officer, Romeo lowered his voice and said, "Let's hear what the guy has to say, before we tell the officer what really happened." I nodded my head in agreement.

Rider lied through his teeth as he recapped everything. He even went as far as saying he saw the guy who took the truck and chased after him on foot but eventually lost him.

I saw Romeo clench his jaw trying not to say anything. Instead of allowing Rider to continue with more lies, Romeo spoke up and told the officer that Rider was moving furniture instead of test-driving the truck.

"That's not true! You're lying." Rider pointed an accusatory finger toward Romeo. But Romeo just smiled and folded his arms across his chest.

"Do you have any proof," the officer asked. Romeo was at a loss for words.

"I do," I chimed in with a smile and pulled out my phone. "I took some photos of him and his friend unloading furniture. I even have a short video, if you want to see it." I held out my phone for the officer and showed him the ninja surveillance proof.

It took a moment for it to set in, but when it finally did Rider spoke up and pointed a finger toward Romeo, again. "So you stole the truck!"

"I didn't steal it. It's mine," Romeo growled. "You drove the truck under false pretenses and lied to us."

"I told you I had to move today and you loaned me the truck," Rider smirked.

By the look on the officer's face, he knew Rider was lying. But the law was the law and he had to cover all bases. "It's his word against yours, Mr. Karr. Unless you have some additional proof," the officer said with his palms up. "There's nothing I can do." Again, Romeo was at a loss for words.

"Yes, we have proof," I said, then all eyes were on me. Rider was going down! "He signed the test-drive form and I have a copy of his drivers license, too. If you want to come back to the lot, I'll show it to you."

Romeo started his badass truck and allowed the rumbling sound of the exhaust system to fill the air before driving away. Rider had to be squirming in the back seat of the police cruiser, trying to think up another lie to get out of trouble.

After seeing the proof, the officer asked Romeo if he wanted to press charges. "No," Romeo said. "But I don't want him back on this lot ever again."

The officer told Rider if he stepped one foot on our property, it would be considered trespassing and he would go directly to jail. Rider got on his motorcycle and left without so much as a "thank you."

"He'll probably go to another lot and do the same thing, if he hasn't finished moving his furniture," Romeo told the officer.

"I'm on it!" I said, then went into the office and began calling the local dealers in our area. I explained to each of them what happened and they thanked me for the information.

After the police officer left, Romeo pulled

me close and gave me a kiss. "What was that for?" I asked.

"For you going the extra mile and making people fill out that form," he said. "I thought it was just a waste of paper. You did good."

"You know, I think you're turning into a badass ninja. Just like me!" I said with a smile. "You were awesome!"

Romeo laughed. "We only have room for one badass ninja. And that would be you, my dear." He kissed me again. "What do you say, we close early and go have some fun?"

"What do you have in mind?" I asked with a sultry smile.

"We could move some furniture around."

Did I miss something? "I don't understand how moving furniture would be fun," I said.

Romeo pulled me closer, and left a trail of tingly kisses from my neck up to my ear. "If things go right, the bed will be moved."

I pulled away, dashed for the office to close up for the day, then yelled over my shoulder, "last one inside buys donuts tomorrow morning!"

Chapter Twenty-Four

HAPPY BIRTHDAY

The tax season refund rush of sales dwindled down and spring warmed the air. Romeo thought I needed help dealing with irrational and impossible people. I wasn't sure what kind of help he thought I needed. If he thought for one second that I needed to see a therapist or take medication, he'd lose that battle.

I did some research on Google and what I discovered just confirmed that stupid would never, ever end. It would never stop. Additional Google searches directed me toward Amazon, where I found some customer service help books that could actually help me. I decided to give the books a chance and hope for the best. It was cheaper than paying a therapist.

When the books arrived, I rushed through them. It turned out running a successful business meant that I had no choice but to deal with screwed up people. That was news to me. I thought I had the right to refuse service to any fucker who pissed me off. One book even suggested that people couldn't drive me crazy as long as I didn't give them the keys. I liked that analogy. It was fitting to the car lot.

I just needed to change my mindset and my attitude toward stupid people. It couldn't be that hard. Maybe I'd been going about this whole customer service thing all wrong. All I had to do was be like the Energizer Bunny on speed and bounce around the car lot with happiness all day long.

Sipping my coffee, I made an important decision. A decision that was so crucial it could alter the rest of my day and possibly the rest of my life. I would weaponize happiness. If I could fake a smile, then I could fake being happy. Forcing happiness on people sounded like a piece of cake compared to leaving my door propped open to the crazies. It was time I did my part to fix stupid. I would go into battle armed with my joyful attitude, spread happiness and beat the snot out of the stupid virus.

I decided that today would be the day I started using the advice I learned from all those customer service guru books. It was time to put that shit to the test. If it didn't work, then I would send an email to all those publishers and demand my money back for selling me false promises. Or I could drink some wine. It was always good to have a backup plan.

I began implementation on my birthday. I was going to be so happy that my cheerful attitude and determination to be happy would force happiness on all those who came in contact with me. I would smile and spread smiles just like Amazon did with their happy boxes. I would laugh and spread laughter, just like those laughing baby videos on YouTube. My inner ninja would spread the happy virus just like the flu, except nobody would get sick. I would not allow anyone to steal my joy today. Nobody was going to ruin my birthday. I was going to be fucking happy if it killed me.

Armed with a smile and a cheerful tone, the first half of my day went surprisingly well. I smiled and laughed and customers smiled and laughed, too. I told stories and managed to answer every phone call with an upbeat voice. I did everything but sing and dance.

I was skeptical about using the advice from

those customer service books, but the suggested techniques were actually working. I was on a roll. Maybe being upbeat and happy was the trick to dealing with stupid people. It was the first time in over a decade that I actually had hope. I might have found the cure to the stupid virus. If my happy attitude could change other people's shitty attitudes, then running our car lot might not be so bad.

That afternoon an older couple followed me into the office. They wanted to discuss a few vehicle prices and made themselves comfortable in my office. The couple's BMW and attire implied they belonged to a higher tax bracket. Perhaps they had important jobs, I wasn't sure, but they had cash to buy without needing to apply for a loan. They were interested in purchasing a car for one of their grandchildren and were asking about a few of the higher end vehicles on our lot.

Cash buyers and people applying for loans were all the same to me. However, it was less paperwork with cash sales, which made my job a lot easier. Happy birthday to me!

Just as we started to discuss prices a much younger couple came into the office. The younger couple noticed the older couple and politely stepped back into the waiting area a few feet away, but I waved them back toward my desk.

It was important to me to acknowledge each person who entered the office so they didn't feel ignored or unwelcome.

"If you have a few questions, I don't mind answering them," I said. "But if you want to test-drive a vehicle, it'll be a few more minutes, before I can get the keys and walk you to the car."

At this point, I expected a few questions or the young man to let me know they wouldn't mind waiting or they'd return in a little while. What I didn't expect was to be rudely interrupted by the older man.

"Excuse me. We were here first," he said, then leaned back in the chair and folded his arms over his chest.

I was stunned, but I smiled anyway. "Yes, but I like to answer people's questions so they don't have to wait."

The old man shifted in his seat and leaned forward.

"But they're black," he whispered with loathing in his voice.

I could feel my birthday happiness slipping away. I, on the other hand, didn't bother to lower my voice.

"That matters why?"

"They can wait."

I glanced toward the lobby, and by the looks on the younger couple's faces, I knew they had heard every word the older man had said. I was ashamed. I was embarrassed. I was just plain mad. My hands balled into fists and it was all I could do not to reach across my desk and strangle the shit out of him.

As I've grown older, I've noticed if someone pissed me off, I enjoyed pissing him or her off even more. Because that was what adults did. And I was an adult. I had to say something because I didn't allow prejudice hatred to carry on around me, nor will I allow it in my office.

I theatrically dropped my pen and pushed my chair away from the desk. I took a deep breath, then looked that old bastard in the eye.

"I'm sorry. I can't help you."

He actually looked confused. "What are you talking about?"

I spun my chair around and pointed to a sign hanging on the wall just behind me and read it out loud. "We reserve the right to refuse service to anyone."

A spark of anger crossed his face. "You can't be serious."

I grinned. This was how the happiness would be spreading today. "Yes, I am. Please show yourselves out."

The old woman's mouth fell open and the old man raised his voice. "I have cash to buy a car!"

"Your money means nothing to me," I replied, because it didn't.

"Do you know who I am?" I noticed a vein pulsing near his temple.

I remained calm. "I don't care who you are."

The old man stood so fast the chair teetered on the back two legs before resting into place. He pointed a warning finger in my direction. "I'll ruin you!" he yelled.

I had had enough of his bullshit. It was past time this fucker learned a valuable lesson, and I felt it was my duty to educate him. I pointed to another sign hanging on the wall that read: Video surveillance. "Not before I upload this video to Facebook, Twitter and the local news stations, including CNN. I might even send it to Oprah. I'll make you famous. Who are you again?"

"You're a bitch!" The old man was fuming now. I had definitely hit a nerve.

I finally lost control of my calm and raised my voice too. "You're a racist bastard! And you're going viral!"

I'd bet all the money in my purse that nobody ever spoke to that old man the way I did or put him in his rightful place. He should really look into some type of brain restoration therapy. I heard it was the new rave—right alongside coffee enemas. His face turned red as he took a deep breath, then slowly released it. He should probably get his blood pressure checked, too.

I didn't know who he was or who he thought he was, but one day I hoped he looked back on this day and realized that he was acting like a fucking idiot. He and his prissy wife stormed past the younger couple in the waiting area and slammed the door on their way out. He probably killed a cricket.

In the back of my mind, I secretly hoped the older couple would buy a car from a crooked car dealer. I imagined him buying a vehicle with no warranty and the engine would go bad within a few weeks. It was probably mean of me to wish bad fortune on them. But I didn't care one fucking bit.

I tried my best to smile as I looked at the younger couple. I couldn't break my new philosophy only hours into day one. I had to be strong and push for positive feelings. Of course that would be easier for me than for them. I couldn't help but notice the tears forming in the young lady's eyes. The young man controlled his composure the best he could, but he was clearly upset, too. I knew they had heard the conversation.

My blood boiled and my hands were shaking. If I didn't get my blood pressure under control, my heart would attack me. It would suck to be in the hospital on my birthday. It was cheaper to calm down and pull my shit together.

I politely excused myself, left the office and made my way toward our home to calm down. Sometimes, I had to walk away and scratch my ass because scratching my head just wasn't good enough. I grabbed a bottle of water out of the refrigerator and walked back toward the office.

I waved the young couple over and gestured toward the empty chairs across from my desk. I chided myself for not spraying the chairs with Lysol before they sat down, because I'd hate for them to catch the stupid virus going around.

I slid the price list directly in front of me, then picked up a pen and tapped it on the desk a few times.

"I'm sorry you had to witness that. I don't normally talk to people in that manner. But I refuse to sell anything to disrespecting assholes who don't give a damn about anyone but themselves. Pardon my language."

The young man glanced at the woman and she nodded. He then looked back at me and said. "Thank you for your honesty. We're here to buy a vehicle and we don't need a loan."

For the next hour, I enjoyed the company of one of the most charming and intelligent young couples I've met in a long time. The young man was some type of engineer, his wife was a nurse and they had recently relocated to our town. After I completed the sale, I gave them each a free t-shirt and they said they'd recommend our car lot to their friends and family.

Having the privilege of meeting that kind young couple, and ending my workday with a smile, was one of the best birthday gifts I could have received.

As I was closing the office, Ginger—my friend and fellow ninja warrior—called to ask if I had any plans for my birthday. I didn't know if Romeo had anything planned, so I told her I'd let her know. It had been a long time since I had a girl's night out, but I didn't want to spoil any of Romeo's possible plans.

When I reached for my phone, it chirped like a cricket, indicating that I had just received a text message from Romeo. It was like he knew I was going to send him a text. The universe must have joined our minds together with some sort of psychic connection or something. It was totally cool. Romeo let me know he had to work mandatory overtime and would be late getting home. But he promised to make it up to me tomorrow. I replied and told him that Ginger wanted to kidnap me for dinner and a movie. Then he responded with kisses and hugs and told me to have fun.

I called Ginger back and she was all about a girl's night out. At our age, that meant dinner and going home early because we both had to work in the morning. Ginger suggested we go to a pizza joint then catch a movie since Romeo would be later than usual, and I agreed. It had been forever since we'd hung out, but I was hungry and she was paying. I wasn't about to turn down free food.

Romeo was home relaxing in front of the television when I returned. He was probably hungry, good thing I brought leftover pizza. Romeo yawned, then stretched his arms above his head.

"Did you have fun?" he asked.

I managed to keep the "pee-pee dance" down to a small wiggle and handed Romeo the pizza box. "I sure did, but I need to visit Sir Johnny fast. 32-ounces of soda is trying to force its way out of my bladder and I'm not wearing a lacy diaper."

I opened the bathroom door and I had to take a step back into the hallway. I rubbed my eyes to make sure I wasn't dreaming, then refocused on what was before me. I swear I heard angels singing. Candles of all different sizes lined every spare area of the bathroom. They were on the sink, in the shower, on the floor and on the windowsill. Pink rose petals blanketed the floor, creating a path, which lead my gaze to one particular location. I covered my mouth with my hands to stop from screaming.

My eyes widened and settled on a big red bow resting on top of the toilet seat. But it wasn't just any toilet seat. No, this toilet seat was connected to the mother of all toilets. It was the badass ninja toilet and it would give us bragging rights in our neighborhood and put all other toilets to shame. In our bathroom sat none other than the super flusher that could flush sixteen golf balls in a single flush, the Champion 4 toilet. I squealed like a little girl on Christmas morning.

On the floor next to the power flusher was a basket filled with different shades of neon golf balls. I wiped away a stray tear as happiness filled my entire being, then started doing a little happy dance and squealed some more.

It was perfect.

Romeo approached me from behind and wrapped his arms around my waist and whispered into my ear, "Happy birthday, Julia."

I turned in Romeo's arms, then pulled him toward me for a long romantic kiss. I grabbed his ass to emphasize just how much I loved it—his ass that is—and the toilet, too. My husband was fucking awesome!

I could barely contain my excitement as Romeo gazed into my eyes. I was expecting him to say something romantic, but instead he asked, "So, what are you going to name this toilet?"

I glanced at the ninja toilet, then back to Romeo. "Sir Johnny 2.0."

Romeo smiled and held up four bags of marshmallows, both large and small, then he nodded toward the champion. "Let's start with these. Shall we?"

I snatched a bag of marshmallows and smiled, "I hope you know. I might never come out of the bathroom. Ever."

Romeo laughed. "It's a good thing we have a second bathroom." I squealed with excitement and did another pee-pee dance.

"Are you ready to flush some balls?" Romeo asked.

"Yes," I said, wishing I had a lacy diaper on.

"But I need to go pee first." So, I jogged to the second bathroom to relieve my bladder.

My toilet dream had finally come true. For the next hour, I wasted a ton of water flushing rose petals, marshmallows and golf balls down Sir Johnny 2.0. Its swooshing power and flushing capabilities left me in awe. Romeo didn't hesitate to snap some photos and record a few videos of me laughing like a crazy woman. I offered to let Romeo flush a few balls, but he insisted he was having more fun watching me.

As ridiculous as it might sound, in that moment I realized that blaming bad customers for who I had become was a victim's mentality, and I was no victim. I was in charge of how I felt. I was in charge of my happiness. I was in charge of my actions and how I behaved. I was a strong and independent woman and I was in charge of my future.

Our business drove me crazy sometimes, from dealing with impossible people with the stupid virus who had no hope for recovery, to the mounds of paperwork piled high on my desk. It was enough to drive a sane person over the edge. But knowing I was a little crazy meant that I wasn't detached from reality. And that made me sane. Thank you Google.

Flushing golf balls down Sir Johnny 2.0 added new entertainment to my already bizarre lifestyle. Some people squeezed stress balls during their workday to relieve tension, but not me. No, I would be the woman flushing golf balls down the toilet. It was the small things in life that mattered and badass ninja toilets and amazing husbands, too. I blamed the car lot.

o

The End

WANT A LITTLE MORE?
TURN THE PAGE FOR...

DISCUSSION QUESTIONS
ABOUT THE AUTHOR
AWARDS

Discussion Questions

Do you have a book club? Below are some discussion questions to get the conversation started:

Do you work in customer service? What is your job?
Have you ever had a bad day at work?
Has a customer ever yelled at you?
Have you ever yelled at a customer?
Have you ever told a customer what you thought?
Have you ever refused service to a customer?
Has a customer every made you cry?
Does your job affect your home life?
Is your job overwhelming at times?
What do you do when you are stressed?
Have you ever wanted to quit your job?
Have you ever been sick and still had to work?
How many hours do you work each week?
Have you ever had an evil Monday?
What was the craziest day you had at work?

About the Author

K.C. is a wife, mother and entrepreneur. She owns and runs a used car lot business and currently resides in the great state of Kentucky with her amazing husband and spoiled dog. K.C.'s husband refers to her as Hobbit size and claims that she is "nuttier than a fruit cake." She owns a complete set of pink tools, believes in aliens and secretly wants to become a badass ninja. In her spare time, she can be found daydreaming about leaving work early to eat chocolate and drink wine. Sometimes her dreams come true.

Awards

CARS, COFFEE, AND A BADASS NINJA TOILET
Best Book Awards Finalist – 2017
Readers' Favorite Five Stars - 2017

THE MAGIC OF FINKLETON
Readers Views Literary Awards – 2011
Readers Favorite Five Stars – 2011
Literary Gold Award – 2011
Literary Classics Finalist – 2011
Children's Literary Classics Seal of Approval – 2011
2012 Next Generation Indie Book Awards – 2012

RETURN TO FINKLETON

Reader's Favorite Five Star Award – 2012
Literary Classics Seal of Approval – 2012
Reader's Favorite Honor Award – 2012
Literary Classics Silver Award – 2012
Reader's Views – Reviewers Choice Awards –
2012

MY NAME IS RAPUNZEL

Children's Literary Classics Silver Award – 2014
Literary Classics Seal of Approval – 2014
Reader's Favorite Gold Award – 2014

www.ingramcontent.com/pod-product-compliance
Lightning Source LLC
Chambersburg PA
CBHW020932120726
47905CB00008B/2480